# 77ZEBRA

Gloria Repp

Greenville, South Carolina

## Library of Congress Cataloging-in-Publication Data

Repp, Gloria, date.
  77 Zebra / by Gloria Repp ; illustrated by David Schuppert.
    p. cm. — (Adventures of an Arctic missionary ; 3)
  Summary: Steve and Liz Bailey continue their work to bring God's
  Word to troubled villagers with the help of their new Cessna airplane.
  ISBN 1-57924-930-2 (alk. paper)
  [1. Missionaries—Fiction. 2. Alaska—Fiction. 3. Christian life—
  Fiction.] I. Schuppert, David, ill. II. Title.
  PZ7.R296Ze 2002
  [Fic]—dc21

                                                            2002154222

Designed by Jamie Miller
Illustrations by David Schuppert

©2003 BJU Press
Greenville, SC 29614

ISBN 1-57924-930-2

15  14  13  12  11  10  9  8  7  6  5  4  3  2  1

*For David Jackson Lohnes,*

*who kept this book alive.*

# Books by Gloria Repp

*The Secret of the Golden Cowrie*
*The Stolen Years*
*Night Flight*
*A Question of Yams*
*Noodle Soup*
*Nothing Daunted*
*Trouble at Silver Pines Inn*
*The Mystery of the Indian Carvings*
*Mik-Shrok*
*Charlie*
*77 Zebra*

# Contents

*Have not I commanded thee?*
*Be strong and of a good courage;*
*be not afraid, neither be thou dismayed:*
*for the Lord thy God is with thee*
*whithersoever thou goest.*
*Joshua 1:9*

# 1  Z Is for Zebra

It looked, at first, like nothing more than a smudge on the horizon, but soon he had no doubt. It was smoke. Steve Bailey turned his attention back to the countless valleys and streams below his small plane. Before he could wonder about that smoke, he had to find the river he would follow. And he'd better make sure it was the right one: the Tiskleet River.

There it was, just a dark thread in a funnel-shaped valley that opened out onto the tundra. At the end of the Tiskleet would be Koyalik, the small Eskimo village where he and Liz had lived last year.

He checked the rows of instruments in front of him and glanced with satisfaction around the plane's snug cockpit. The winter of 1950 was one they'd never forget, but this year would be better. The weather would be cold and stormy, of course; you expect that in Alaska Territory. But having a plane would enable them to get around more easily. It would make all the difference in the world to their work.

Below, the land had flattened into treeless tundra that was brown and gold, dotted with lakes. The winding Tiskleet River flashed and sparkled in the sun. Last winter he'd used the frozen river as a highway for his dogsled trips to Shanaluk, and farther north, to Mierow Lake. Today he would land on it.

He kept an eye on the smoke. It was closer now, a roiling gray-black column that rose high over the tundra, as if someone were sending up a plea for help.

Beside him, his wife watched it too. Her small face, usually so cheerful, was shadowed with worry. "Straight ahead of us," she said. "Is it at Koyalik?"

"Could be." Steve folded up the chart he'd been using. Black smoke usually meant trouble, like rubber or gasoline burning. What was happening at Koyalik? They'd soon find out.

The river grew wide as it flowed past willow thickets and meandered around sandbars. It would swell into a small lagoon beside Koyalik, then empty into the ocean and become part of Norton Sound.

"We're almost there." He picked up the radio microphone. "Galena radio, this is Cessna 1577 Zebra. We're crossing the Tiskleet River south of Koyalik. I'd like to close my flight plan."

"Roger, 77 Zebra," said a voice on the radio.

Liz leaned against her seat belt to peer through the windshield. "Do you think they got our letter? Will they be waiting for us with—"

"With an Eskimo brass band?" Steve grinned. "Well, they'll have to wait a little longer. I don't think we're going any lower until we take a look at that smoke."

"The first thing I want to find out is how Charlie's doing. Do you think he'll be there?"

"I sure hope so."

Charlie: the Eskimo teenager who'd been on their hearts and in their prayers ever since they'd met him last winter. He was bright-eyed, smart, and adventuresome, but not the least bit interested in knowing God. It had been hard to leave him, even for the summer.

Now they could see Koyalik. Flames blazed high from a dirty-gray cloud at one end of the tiny airstrip, and smoke drifted over the village. Small figures ran around the edges of the fire, hurrying from it to the ocean and back again.

Steve made a wide circle over the village, then circled again at a lower altitude. Several cabins near the airstrip seemed to be on fire . . . or at least, their roofs were burning. Did sod roofs burn more slowly than wooden ones? He didn't know.

Liz glanced at him. "We can still land, can't we?"

"Yes, since we're on floats, we can land on the river. It's a fairly safe distance away."

He banked steeply, tipping the airplane on its left wing as he flew low over the river to check for obstacles. He'd taken lessons to get his seaplane rating after they'd picked up the airplane in San Francisco, but he still wasn't comfortable with landing on water. "Watch it now," he muttered to himself. "Water rudders up. Carb heat on. Adjust trim tab."

The plane slid down onto the river with a spray of water, and he taxied up to a sandbar near the bank. He shut down the engine, stepped out of the cockpit onto one of the plane's floats, and jumped down onto the sand. While Liz was still climbing out of the plane, he pounded a stake into the gravelly sand and knotted a tie-down rope to it. Although they were at the south edge of the village, he could smell smoke, and the sky over their heads was a haze of gray.

They splashed through shallow water to the riverbank, wearing knee-high rubber boots. Even in September, the water would be bone-chillingly cold.

"Could you stay with the plane until I find out what's going on?" he asked Liz. "I don't want any kids jumping on it."

"Steve, a warm welcome for you!" A sooty-faced Eskimo with sparkling black eyes pounded him on the shoulder.

Steve grinned at the man who was Charlie's father and the only Eskimo in Koyalik who had become a Christian.

"Tignak! Good to see you! What can I do to help?"

"Well, we've got a sort of bucket system going. The wind blew the fire down onto the cabins, but they'll be all right if we can keep them wet. It's the tundra we're worried about. If the fire spreads out there, it'll go underground and burn forever. Come on back to the airstrip with me. I'll show you."

Fire still burned on the runway, and the wind swirled heat and suffocating smoke into Steve's face. Men and women were using caribou skins to beat out flames in the grass, and children were running up and down the slope with buckets of water.

A tall, lean figure stepped through the smoke and shouted at him. "Steve! Welcome back!"

It was Gus Svenson, village schoolteacher and owner of the Trading Post. His face, usually white and pink, was gray with soot, and flecks of ash darkened his gray beard. "Good timing!" he exclaimed. He handed Steve a shovel. "Come on over here. We can use some muscle on this fire line."

Steve joined the men at the edge of the tundra who were uprooting bushes and scraping back the grass. He and Gus worked with them for the next hour, shoveling debris out of the way to make a wide corridor of bare earth.

The fire sank lower and finally died out.

Steve flexed his aching shoulders and watched the children who had run up to splash water across the fire line. Beside him, Gus leaned on his shovel, breathing hard. "Just one cigarette butt in the grass," the old trader muttered. "That's all it took."

"And a fuel drum?" Steve wiped at his eyes, still watering from the smoke.

"Yah. The grass caught fire and spread to an empty drum lying on its side. It exploded, sending pieces of metal into a full drum—and suddenly we had a huge fire on our hands." Gus's eyes were red-rimmed and weary. "We wanted to keep it away from the cabins and the tundra. Well, we did."

The village men gathered round, smiles of welcome brightening their soot-stained, sweating faces.

Steve smiled back. "It feels as if we've been gone for years instead of only three months," he said. "How's everything going?"

"New room on Trading Post," said one old man. "We help Gus build it."

"They sure did," said Gus. "And I finally got a permit to put in a ground-to-air radio. Might come in handy with that airplane of yours around."

"Village doing fine," said another.

The man named Henry frowned. "Except for new pilot."

Tignak was frowning too. "There's a new guy who takes turns with Jackson flying the mail. I guess the route has been expanded. He goes by the name of Mack. We think his cigarette butt started the fire."

Steve shook his head in sympathy. "Anyone get hurt?"

"No, I'm thankful to say. A lot of people are still at fish camp or up the river somewhere," said Tignak.

"I suppose Victor's at fish camp too?" He and Liz had prayed all summer for the friendly young Eskimo who had been their translator when they first came to Koyalik.

There was a silence. Tignak glanced at Victor's uncle. Victor's uncle looked at the ground, and his cheerful face dimmed. "Victor a little bit sick these days."

Steve scraped some dirt off his shovel. Best not to ask any more about Victor right now. Sounded like he wasn't doing any better than when they'd left. Well, that's why they had come back.

He gazed down through the village, and the sun glinting on the river reminded him that he'd left Liz there with the Cessna.

He smiled at his friends. "Come and see the plane the Lord gave us."

They walked along the wide lane that ran between a row of log cabins. Near each cabin stood a log hut built on stilts, a cache hut used for storing the winter's supply of food. Brightly colored washing waved from clotheslines, and salmon and whale skins hung on dooryard racks, drying. Steve breathed in the odors of salt air, fish, and wood smoke and felt that he had come home.

The lane branched right, leading to the tall building that was the Trading Post. "I need to clean up," said Gus. "We'll get together soon, Steve, and you can tell me all about your summer." He turned toward the Trading Post, and Steve continued on with Tignak. The old Eskimo, well-educated and wise in the ways of his people, had become one of his best friends in Koyalik.

"Where's Charlie?" asked Steve. "Oh, there he is."

Tignak's son stood at the edge of the river, talking to Liz. Charlie looked as alert and energetic as Steve remembered. He'd grown, though; now he was taller than Liz.

"He's sure missed you two," said Tignak. "Keeps talking about the trips you took with him. And about that airplane you'd be bringing back."

Steve smiled. *And I missed you, Charlie,* he thought.

When they reached the riverbank, Charlie swung around, grabbed Steve's hand, and shook it vigorously. "Gimme some skin! Gimme some skin!" He stepped back, a smile lighting his serious face. "We get your letter. I hope you come today. We have feast, just for you. My fadder and I get *oogruk*—a seal."

He pointed at the Cessna, which bobbed gently at the edge of the sandbar. "I like your plane. Red and white good." He read out the plane's numbers with satisfaction. "1-5-7-7-Z. And Z is for zebra; that what pilots say, right? But zebra need black stripes."

"Wait until you see the inside, boy." Steve grinned at Liz and then at Charlie.

"Can go look now?"

"Sure." Steve glanced down at Charlie's sealskin boots. "The water's not very deep."

Once they reached the plane, Steve gave Charlie a boost up onto a float, then climbed up himself and opened the cockpit door.

Charlie peered inside and grinned. "Hey! Look like zebra in there."

"It sure does. The seats were in bad shape, so Liz found some cloth with black and white stripes and made new covers."

Steve crawled into the plane and leaned over the back seat. "Here, want to carry a couple of suitcases for us?"

Since most of their supplies were coming by boat, it didn't take long to empty the small plane. Willing hands helped carry everything up to the cabin they had left three months before. The door had no lock, as was customary in the village, and Tignak opened it with a flourish.

Liz took a step into the cabin and stopped short. "A new table! It's nice and long. Where's our old—oh, Steve, look!"

Their old table stood to the left of the doorway under the window, but now it had a polished wood top. Beside it was a chair upholstered with moose hide.

"A place to study," said Tignak.

Charlie plopped down in the new chair and hunched over the table; then he grinned up at Steve. "Do homework good!"

"Guess I won't have an excuse now," said Steve. "This is great!"

"And here's a bench for our new table!" Liz exclaimed. "Now we'll have room for lots of visitors." She turned, her face glowing. "I love it! Who did this?"

"People worked together," said Tignak.

"And everything's so clean!"

"That was Sarah's idea," said Tignak. "Then we all helped."

His ten-year-old daughter stood quietly beside an old woman, their grandmother. Sarah didn't say anything, but her black eyes shone.

"You!" Liz bent down to give her a hug. "I missed you, Sarah. We need to have a long talk, just you and me."

Sarah nodded and whispered something that Steve couldn't hear.

"A secret? Good. I hope you'll tell me soon."

"The dogs!" Steve suddenly remembered them. "How are the dogs, Charlie?"

"Bandit get sick, but he better now," said Charlie. "The rest do fine. Mikki smart as ever. Come see."

He had chained Steve's huskies with the others behind Tignak's house. The dogs lay asleep, stretched out in the sun. Bigfoot, their big brown dependable worker, raised his head lazily. Howler, thin as ever, opened one eye. Bandit didn't move a muscle.

"They've forgotten us," said Liz. "I was afraid of that."

A gray husky at the far end of the line scrambled to his feet. He lifted his beautiful white-masked face, cocked one ear, and stared at them, trembling.

"Mikki," said Steve, and the dog began to whine.

Charlie ran to unsnap the chain.

Mikki charged at Steve, almost knocking him over. Steve knelt to welcome him, and the heavy muzzle with its cold nose burrowed into Steve's neck.

He scratched behind the floppy ear. "Have you been good?" he whispered. "Have you behaved for Charlie?" He put both arms around the dog's neck and felt the powerful muscles ripple as Mikki leaned into him.

Liz, kneeling beside them, crooned in the special voice she used, and Mikki turned to nuzzle her, licking her throat and face until she laughed and backed away in self-defense. "This one didn't forget!"

Finally Steve stood up and brushed himself off. "Well, I guess we'll take Mikki over to the cabin with us." He looked at Charlie. "Would you like to keep the other three for your own? Since we have the Cessna, we probably won't use a dog team very much. Maybe we could borrow your team for hauling wood and water."

Charlie drew himself up to his full height. "Would like very much indeed." He sounded so much like Tignak that Steve almost laughed aloud.

Tignak smiled at them both. "He's been wanting his own team for a long time, but well-trained dogs are expensive. This will get him off to a good start."

"Come back to our cabin," said Liz. She waved to Sarah and the grandmother, who were watching from the corner of the cabin. "I'll fix us something to eat, and we can get caught up on the news."

"But Sarah . . ." Charlie looked at his sister.

"Yes," said Tignak. "Sarah will roast us alive if you don't come to our cabin for supper. She's got it all planned."

"In that case—" Liz glanced up at the sky.

A plane buzzed in a wide circle over the village. Tignak shaded his eyes to watch it. "Hmm . . . the mail plane. It should be Jackson. We got that fire off the runway just in time."

# 2 Warfare

"Sure am glad you invited me to the welcome party." Jackson helped himself to fried seal liver and another piece of boiled ground squirrel, then poured gravy over everything on his plate. He rubbed at the scar that curved down one side of his face. "It's been a long summer."

"What I want to know," said Liz, "is why you shaved off your mustache."

"Too hot. And I was tired of looking dignified." He grinned at Sarah and Charlie. "The kids like it better this way."

Sarah smiled up at the tall blond pilot. "Tell story again, please, for the World War Two. How face gets cut." She glanced at Steve and Liz. "Every time he come eat at our house, I say he have to tell story. He tell lots of stories this summer."

Jackson shrugged. "Okay, then, if that's still the rule." He put down his fork. "Well, I was flying a 4F Wildcat that day, and there were about six of us. The sky was full of Japanese Zeros. I shot down one of 'em, and then I headed for another one, but it looped away from me. I twisted up behind it, rolled upside down, and took a shot. It burst into flames.

"As soon as I leveled out, I saw a Zero diving past me. I rammed the stick forward and went after it. I caught up with it pretty fast and scored some shots, but another Zero came

at me out of a cloud, and all of a sudden my Wildcat began to shake, and I knew I'd been hit."

Jackson picked up his fork, his blue eyes twinkling. "You know the rest."

"No," said Sarah. "Tell all, please."

"Well . . . the engine died, so I put my plane into a long shallow dive, hoping to land somewhere close to the base. But another Zero swooped past me and sent some bullets through my canopy. Shattered it all to pieces. I remember trying to get my parachute up, and the next thing I knew, I was in the water.

"I drank a lot of sea water while I got untangled from the ropes and inflated my life vest. Then I inflated the life raft and managed to crawl onto it. That's when I noticed that blood was dripping down the side of my face. Must have been hit by a piece of the canopy."

He stopped to take a drink of tea.

"And then," said Charlie.

"And then I spotted some shark fins in the water just a couple feet away. I got the chlorine powder out of my emergency pack and sprinkled a lot of it into the water. I watched those sharks real close, I can tell you, but after a few minutes they disappeared. Then I must have passed out for a while. When I came to, it was getting dark, and I could hear the searchers looking for me. They finally hauled me out of the life raft, and I got back to my base okay."

Sarah smiled. "And now you have shot down five Zeros, and so Captain Jackson is Ace pilot."

"And so you win the war," added Charlie with satisfaction.

"Well, we won the battle of Guadalcanal," said Jackson. "That was back in 1942, and we weren't at all sure we were going to win the war. We had a lot of battles ahead of us."

"But you fight hard and the United States of America win World War Two." Sarah looked as proud as if she had shot down an enemy plane herself. She handed Jackson a plate of black, rubbery-looking meat. "Want more *muktuk?*"

"Sure do." Jackson took a strip of the Eskimo delicacy and cut it up into squares on his plate.

Steve helped himself to a strip too, and spread it with mustard. Muktuk was raw whale skin with its blubber still attached, and even though it looked odd, he thought it tasted like roast beef. But he'd never have the nerve to eat it Eskimo-style, the way Charlie did.

Charlie took a strip of muktuk from the plate, clamped his teeth onto one end, and stretched it out with his left hand. With the other hand, he slashed downward with his knife, slicing the strip in two, and began chewing. The four-inch blade had passed less than an inch from his nose, but no one seemed concerned.

Jackson speared a biscuit with his fork. "Good biscuits."

"Missus Lizzie teach me," said Sarah.

Jackson nodded. "Guess we're all glad you guys are back," he said. "They even fired up the airstrip for you!"

Steve grinned. "I think that was an accident. But what's this I hear about a new pilot working the mail route?"

Charlie sliced off another bite of muktuk and looked at Jackson as if he were wondering too.

"Mack?" said Jackson. "The company is expanding, and they took him on. He flew during the war too, and you'd think we could be friends, but something about that boy makes me jumpy."

Tignak murmured in agreement, and Jackson went on. "They're hiring all kinds, these days. The aviation business is booming—has been ever since the war. The Air Force is even planning to put in some radar installations along the coast."

"I read about that," said Steve.

"Not a bad idea." Jackson glanced at Tignak. "Speaking of the Air Force, I heard an interesting story the other day. Friend of mine was talking about a tractor—one of those big cats—that's been abandoned somewhere east of Nome. Belongs to the Air Force, but it needs repair, and they don't want it."

"So why is your eagle eye fixed on me?" asked Tignak. "You think I want a tractor that doesn't run?"

Jackson threw back his head and laughed. "I think you and Charlie could fix it if you wanted to. And it might come in handy around the village here."

Tignak exchanged a look with his son.

"Aha!" said Jackson. "I know what that means. Maybe I can find out some more about it." He glanced at his watch. "Come to think of it, I have to get back to Nome this afternoon. If I can find the right people, I'll ask some questions about that tractor."

He stood up and pulled on his leather flight jacket. "I sure do like your Cessna, Steve. If the weather holds, I'll fly the Cub down on Saturday and give you a hand building that pier." He bowed to Sarah. "My compliments to the cook."

After Jackson left, Charlie mumbled, "Pier. What is pier?"

"Oh," said Steve, "when I was showing Jackson my plane, we talked about the best way to keep it tied down. We'll need some kind of a pier, he told me. That's like a platform built at the edge of the river."

"But river wash it away in storm," said Charlie, chewing steadily.

"Right. Before you can build a pier, you have to put in pilings—that's long pieces of wood or iron pounded into the ground. Then you'll have a strong base for your pier."

Tignak sliced off a bite of muktuk. "I think I've seen some old pilings down there. You might want to use them."

"That would save a lot of work," said Steve. "You'll have to show me where they are. Maybe they're left from when they built the airstrip during the war."

"I will help pier," said Charlie. He pushed his plate back, wiped his knife on his sleeve, and studied the blade. Then he took a small whetstone from his pocket and began stroking the knife with it.

While Charlie sharpened his knife and the women did the dishes, Steve and Tignak talked about the situation in Koyalik. "It's been quiet," Tignak said. "Like I said, most people move to fish camp or hunt squirrels or go somewhere else during the summer. Only a couple of families came to the services. But I've been studying those books you sent me. Mr. Spurgeon certainly was some preacher! On Sundays I practice on anyone who shows up."

"Good for you," said Steve. "What's happening in Shanaluk?" Last year, he and Liz had made several trips to the village where Tignak used to live, but Am-nok, the shaman there, had done everything he could to oppose them.

"Am-nok still holds their hearts and minds," Tignak said with a frown. "I went back a few times this summer, but even when I spoke to my friend Joseph, I felt as if I were talking to myself."

"I know what you mean," said Steve. "I felt a lot of resistance when I preached there, and I'm sure Am-nok was behind it." As he thought about the shaman, Jackson's story came to mind, and the opposition in Shanaluk took on new meaning.

*We're in a warfare here,* he thought. *Not World War II, but a spiritual warfare.*

To Tignak, he said, "Now that we have the Cessna, we can hop up there for a visit and be back the same day. I think there's a lake to land on. Let's plan a trip for—let's see— how about tomorrow afternoon?"

He glanced at Liz. They had plenty of settling in to do, but she knew how important Shanaluk was to him.

She smiled back, and Tignak said, "That sounds good to me." The frown on his forehead smoothed out. "Maybe the weather will stay clear."

Charlie looked anxious. "Is room for me?"

"Sure," said Steve. "If you help me gas up the plane, I'll let you be my copilot."

The next day after lunch, Charlie helped Steve roll a 55-gallon drum of aviation gas up to the Cessna.

"Okay, hop up onto the wing," said Steve.

Charlie grinned and scrambled up onto the drum, then onto the plane's wing.

Steve unscrewed the gas cap from the wing tank, and in the opening he set a large funnel covered with a piece of chamois skin. "You might as well sit down," he said. "This will take a while."

Charlie sat with his legs dangling over the edge of the wing, and Steve handed him one end of the tubing that attached to a hand pump on the drum. "Hold that down in the funnel and tell me when it starts filling up with gas."

He began turning the crank on the hand pump, and Charlie stared into the funnel. "Too much," he said suddenly, and Steve stopped cranking for a minute.

"What for we do this?" asked Charlie.

"To strain out any water or rust that got into the gas," said Steve. "Bad gas can wreck the engine."

It took more than an hour to fill both wing tanks, and then Steve showed Charlie how to check the floats and clean out the water that had leaked into them.

"Water make plane too heavy?"

"Right," said Steve. "Even a little bit can upset the plane's balance and make it crash."

Finally the plane was ready and the preflight check had been done. Steve made sure Tignak and Charlie had their seat belts on, then he swung the airplane around and started his takeoff run down the river. Charlie exclaimed in delight as water sprayed high on both sides, and suddenly they were airborne.

They climbed to gain altitude. Koyalik fell away beneath them until the river looked like just a trickle of water across the flat landscape. Steve filed a flight plan, and it seemed he had hardly finished before they were passing over a group of cabins huddled on the tundra. He pointed down at them. "Shanaluk."

"But so small." Charlie pressed close to the window. "Shanaluk? You sure?"

"I think so," Steve said. They'd been flying for less than a half hour, but Shanaluk was only forty miles away, so that would be right. "Now where's that lake?"

Charlie gave a yelp of discovery. "There, on other side."

Steve eyed the small round lake. It might be big enough. "Let's check it out."

Charlie's head swung back and forth as he watched every move Steve made and tried to look out the window at the same time.

Steve closed his flight plan and concentrated on landing. He circled the lake and made a low pass over the water, looking for logs or anything that could damage the plane's floats. Then he set up an approach and carefully put the plane down onto the lake. There was no pier, of course, but there was a sloping beach, and after anchoring the plane, they splashed to shore.

A group of men soon gathered at the edge of the village, friends of Tignak's that Steve recognized from last year. Joseph didn't seem to be around. Steve talked with them, feeling awkward with his rusty Eskimo. They discussed the weather, and he asked about their families. Tignak took a turn at speaking, and the conversation picked up speed.

Steve listened to the complicated, rippling Eskimo words and gazed down through the village. People seemed to be coming in and out of one particular cabin more than any of the others. Where had Charlie disappeared to?

When Tignak finished, no one asked any questions. The men nodded politely and walked away. Tignak turned to Steve. "There is trouble here, and these people are not interested in what we have to say. Charlie has gone to find out what he can."

They strolled through the village, greeting each man they passed. Joseph was working outside his cabin, caulking the logs with moss, and Steve hurried over to talk to him. Joseph did not seem in the mood for visiting. He answered Steve's questions with a brief "yes" or "no," as if his mind were on other things.

Finally, they turned back toward the airplane, and a few minutes later Charlie caught up with them. He exchanged a few sentences with his father in rapid Eskimo, then trudged ahead in silence.

The sky was heavily overcast by the time they took off, and Steve decided to stay below the clouds and follow the river back to Koyalik. The rough air made for a bumpy ride, but Charlie didn't seem to notice. His face was blank. What was bothering him, Steve wondered. It seemed that the boy had gone away to a place where he could not follow.

After they landed near the sandbar at Koyalik, Charlie lunged out of the airplane and splashed hurriedly to shore.

Steve pulled out the tie-down rope from behind his seat. He looked inquiringly at Tignak.

"There is grief at Shanaluk," Tignak said slowly. "Their shaman is dying. They believe that only the spell of another shaman could make Am-nok sicken as he has. You saw the people coming and going from Am-nok's cabin? They are unhappy and afraid. Charlie is too. Am-nok is still very important to him."

Sadness crossed the old Eskimo's dark, angular face. "I hope you're praying for Charlie. Sometimes that boy is so miserable, he doesn't even want to go hunting."

He took the rope Steve handed him and pulled the plane close to the sandbar. After they'd tied down the plane, he smiled a little. "Did Sarah tell you her good news yet? No? She will soon, I think."

Late that afternoon, wind rushed in from the sea, growing stronger and stronger by the moment. Steve went out several times to check on his plane, and by evening, the little Cessna was bouncing in the waves, tugging at the rope that held it down. Should he get it out of the river?

A picture filled his mind of another small plane tossing on the water, a plane that had been torn to pieces by an Alaskan storm. Peter, the missionary who had started the work at Koyalik, had been the pilot of that plane. Now Peter was in San Francisco, still trying to recover from his injuries.

Steve turned and ran to the Trading Post for help.

An hour later, four men had pulled the Cessna up onto the beach so Steve could tie it down more securely. He made sure the nose was facing into the wind and looped the tie-down ropes, one for each wing, around a pair of 55-gallon drums filled with beach gravel.

He lay awake most of the night, thinking about the plane. Rain pounded against the windows, and he wondered how strong the storm would get. Would the wind shift direction? Would the tie-down ropes hold? He'd seen planes flip in the wind and end up with a bent propeller or torn wings. That was damage he couldn't fix by himself.

Toward morning he put on his rubber slicker and boots and sloshed down through the sleeping village to make sure the ropes were still attached. In the beam of his flashlight, the plane looked okay. It swayed in the wind, but it was secure.

"Thank you, Lord," he murmured, not minding the cold rain in his face, and went back to bed.

The storm blew all the next day, but by Thursday afternoon it quieted, and Gus predicted that the mail plane would make its usual run. Steve heard a plane circling beneath the clouds, and he decided to go down to the airstrip. He could meet the new pilot and give him a friendly welcome.

The pilot climbed slowly out of the plane, glanced at Steve, and stepped to the baggage compartment. He was tall and lean, and he wore high-topped leather boots and a brown leather flight jacket, like most pilots who had fought in World War II.

He started unloading boxes from the crowded interior, moving swiftly and efficiently. By now, a few Eskimo children had gathered, but they watched in silence. If Jackson were here, Steve thought, they'd be all over him. And they'd carry this stuff up to the Trading Post for him.

He moved to the stack of boxes. "Need a hand?"

The pilot straightened to his full height, took off his sunglasses, and looked Steve over. Beneath long black hair, his eyes were very blue, and they held a look of contempt. But all he said was, "Okay. Just don't drop anything."

After they reached the Trading Post and piled their boxes in the storeroom, Steve gave him a smile. "I'm Steve Bailey. And you must be Mack?"

"Yeah. You're the missionary." Mack turned and started back to the airstrip. Over his shoulder, he said, "Just stay out of my way and we'll get along fine."

# 3 Little Yellow Spot

The stormy weather persisted, but on Saturday morning, Jackson's Piper Cub spun down out of the clouds like a yellow leaf, and Steve hurried to meet him at the airstrip.

Tignak, Charlie, and several others had already stacked peeled spruce logs beside the old pilings, and together they set to work building a pier.

Gus strolled down from the Trading Post to watch, and he stayed to help lift the heavy logs into place. He nodded with approval as the pier took shape. "This will be useful for the whole village. Yah, Steve, you make good things happen around here."

He clapped Steve on the back and went back to the Trading Post, but his words left a warm glow behind, and Steve whistled to himself as he reached for the saw.

While they were finishing up, Jackson said to Tignak, "By the way, that tractor is yours if you want it. Talked to one of the men up there and got official permission." He drawled the last two words with smiling emphasis. "Found out where it is too."

Charlie's head jerked up, and he grinned at his father.

Tignak looked thoughtful. "I wonder how long it would take us to get there."

Jackson smiled. "I'd take you in my plane, but I only have room for one passenger. Now Steve here has a flying hotel. He can take three passengers. Or you could walk. Maybe get there in a week or two."

"Hmmm," said Steve. "Are you guys doing this just to make me feel wanted?"

Even Tignak laughed at that. But then he said, "Look, Steve, your plane belongs to the Mission, and if you don't think . . ."

Steve picked up his hammer and the long crosscut saw. "What I think is that you've done plenty for the Mission, and I'd be glad to help you out." He glanced at Jackson. "You figure a couple of hours?"

"Unless you get lost."

"That's a happy thought. Would you like to be my third passenger?"

Jackson grinned. "If y'all don't mind waiting until next Saturday. Sounds like an adventure."

They tied the Cessna to the new pier and went up to Steve's cabin for lunch. Over bowls of thick fish soup, they discussed their plans.

"You think we see bears up there?" Charlie looked hopeful.

"Sure don't want to," said Jackson. "Maybe they'll all be off eating berries or something. Took me the whole summer to get a decent patch on my Cub from the last bear we met. Speaking of the great Alaskan wilderness, Steve, what do you have for emergency gear?"

"Just the basics."

"Okay." Jackson took another handful of round pilot crackers to dunk in his soup. "You want to have enough stuff to survive in the wilderness for at least a week. Got a pencil, Liz?"

She reached over to Steve's desk. "I have one right here."

"You'll bring your tools, of course. And pack some oatmeal, dried peas, dried soup, raisins, powdered milk, and canned meat. Then you'll need fishhooks, and tackle, and a needle and thread. A small camp stove with extra fuel. Plenty of candles. Your rifle and extra shells, matches, a pot or two, sleeping bags, and a tent."

Liz put down her pencil. "That's not too bad. We've got most of it already."

"I was thinking we should get a better tent," Steve said.

"Don't buy one. Even the best store-bought tent will crack at forty degrees below zero when you unfold it." Jackson looked so serious that Steve suspected it had happened to him.

The pilot glanced at Liz. "I saw those seat covers you made for the Cessna. Get some balloon cloth, and you can make your own tent. An Eskimo woman made mine for me, just after the war ended. That was six years ago, and it's still in good shape. I'll show it to you."

That afternoon, clouds slid across the sky, and Jackson left before they dropped any lower. By evening, wind howled through the village, and rain was blowing sideways in icy gusts. Huge waves thundered in from the sea.

Once again, the men helped Steve pull the Cessna out of the river, and this time he moved it farther away from the water. The drums weighted with gravel seemed solid enough, but he filled them with water to add even more weight.

"Five-day storm," said Victor's uncle. The wind snatched his words away, and he had to hang onto the plane to keep from being blown down. The gusts were so strong that none of them could stand upright without support.

Sunday, the storm still blew, and no one came to the service at Tignak's cabin. Monday, the wind rose to gale force, and the mail plane did not show up. The river churned with whitecaps and surged high up onto the beach.

The wind rattling at their windows and stovepipe reminded Steve again and again that Peter's plane had been destroyed during a storm. That was a different situation, since it had been moored on a lake, but still . . .

"Lord, this plane is Your property," he prayed. "Keep it safe if You will." He checked on the Cessna several times each day, and one blustery night he had to tighten the ropes, but the little plane stayed secure.

Since the storm kept almost everyone indoors, Steve decided that this would be a good time to get re-acquainted with the people of Koyalik. He and Liz visited one family after another. Each family received them politely and served them hot black tea. They dried their rain-soaked clothes beside the stove, which was kept roaring hot, and learned the names of all the children.

Liz was better at talking than he was, so Steve usually let her begin a friendly attempt at conversation. Some people spoke broken English and some spoke none at all, but most seemed to understand what Liz was saying. Steve drank his tea and smiled and put in a word now and then.

While he listened, he asked the Lord to open his heart to the needs of his people. He noticed the amulets they wore and their careful observance of taboos. He saw the weary, downcast faces and the sadness in the dark eyes. Sometimes he could feel the despair and hopelessness of an old man or woman who was unable to get out of bed.

*Tignak is right,* he thought, remembering what the old Eskimo had told him. *These people live in fear.*

Each evening, he and Liz prayed specifically for the families they had visited that day. "I'm understanding more and more how darkness and fear rule their lives," Steve said to Liz one night. "Only God's power can change that, but it's going to be a battle."

"I know what you mean," she said slowly. "It's kind of a scary thought that we're up against the powers of darkness here."

When they weren't visiting, he and Liz worked together on the new tent. Gus had found some white balloon cloth in his storeroom and an Eskimo woman to give them advice. He suggested that they sew wide black stripes onto the tent so it would be easier to see from the air, and Steve thought that was a good idea.

Charlie saw what they were doing. "You make zebra tent!" he exclaimed with a laugh.

In the middle of the week, they resumed their Eskimo lessons with Tignak. "You've forgotten a lot over the summer," said Tignak. "But it will come back if you stick to it. Try to use your Eskimo as much as you can."

Steve looked over the list in his vocabulary notebook, remembering how hard they had worked last fall to collect Eskimo words. He nudged Liz and pointed to the word for a bearded seal. "Remember oogruk, when Victor took us hunting for whales and I thought it meant 'look there' "?

She laughed. "Victor was such a help to us," she said to Tignak. "We practiced all our new words on him, and we must have sounded awful."

"He probably thought we'd never learn them," said Steve, "but Victor is one of the most patient men I know."

He looked at Tignak. "I keep watching for him, but he doesn't seem to have come back to the village yet. Is he still sick? What's he got?"

Tignak's face darkened. "He's got a case of *tong-nuk.*"

"What's that?"

"It's a kind of home-brewed beer. He makes it up there at his fish camp and—what's the word?—guzzles it down. I've talked to him a couple times, but he doesn't listen."

"Where's Nida?" asked Liz.

"His wife went to stay with her sister in Nome."

Steve felt a hollow sadness. Victor had translated his preaching all last fall, so he had heard sermon after sermon filled with God's Word.

Slowly he turned the water-stained page in his notebook. "I'm going to keep praying for Victor. He's been a good friend."

The storm hung on until almost the end of the week, but to the relief of the whole village, it left in time for the supply boat's arrival on Friday. Besides Steve and Liz's luggage, the small freighter brought them twenty drums of aviation gas from the Mission.

Saturday morning, Jackson arrived right on schedule, and after they'd tied up his Piper Cub, they loaded 77 Zebra for the trip north.

"I'll bring my survival gear," said Jackson, "since yours isn't quite ready. Tignak, do you need any tools for fixing that tractor?"

"I have a few," said Tignak. "And plenty of wire. That should do me."

Charlie seemed quieter than usual, but perhaps he was just thinking about the tractor. He sat beside Tignak in the back seat and flattened his nose against the window.

The sky had a high overcast, but the hills north of Koyalik were tinted bronze and rusty red, and their colors lighted up the gray afternoon.

Steve took off into the wind, lifting one wing to break the suction of the water, and Jackson smiled, approving. "Glad to see they taught you that little trick. Good way to pick up air speed when you're on one of those tiny lakes."

Steve set a course north by northeast, filed his flight plan, then picked up the chart in his lap. "Not much here to go on, is there?" he said. "It looks as if they haven't gotten around to mapping the Interior yet."

Jackson shrugged. "They will someday. I like to fly dead reckoning anyway, because then I know where I am. You get so you recognize the different hills and lakes and rivers."

He glanced out his window. "For example, down there's a branch of the Tiskleet that I use. See it?"

Steve banked the plane to take a good look at the river that snaked across the tundra toward the mountains. "Got it."

The land unrolled beneath them, tundra wrinkling into valleys, deep ravines, and mountains. Already the high ridges were dusted with snow.

Steve studied the rugged terrain. There didn't seem to be many places to make an emergency landing. Maybe one of those lakes.

"There's another checkpoint you can use," Jackson was saying. He pointed to a mountain peak with a distinctive square top that slanted off to one side. "They call it Old Man's Hat, and I look for it whenever I fly this route."

"Okay." Steve took note of where Old Man's Hat was situated in relation to the river. He'd certainly be flying this way again. Mierow Lake, a settlement of English-speaking Eskimos that he'd preached in last year, was a little farther east of the route they were flying now. He and Liz had already made plans to go back to Mierow Lake next week.

Tignak was paying careful attention to the terrain below, and Steve knew he was memorizing it for the trip back. If they did get the tractor working again, he and Charlie would have to drive it all the way back to Koyalik. Their baggage, stacked behind the back seat, included supplies for at least three weeks.

Soon Jackson pointed out a lake, and Steve circled lower to check it out. A faint road rambled off from the lake shore, losing itself in the forest.

Jackson raised his voice so Tignak could hear above the noise of the engine. "See that road? Your tractor's at the end of it. Let's go take a look."

Steve tilted the airplane so Tignak, sitting behind him, could get a better view, and they flew low over the trees.

"I see it," Tignak said.

"Where?" Steve made another circle. There was the road. And plenty of trees. Nothing else that he could see.

Charlie had crawled over to look out Tignak's window, almost sitting in his father's lap. "Yes!" he shouted. "Little yellow spot."

Steve finally caught a glimpse of yellow beneath the trees and leveled out the plane. "Okay. Let's get you down there."

It didn't take long to unload the supplies and wish the travelers well. Tignak and Charlie were already setting up camp when Steve made his takeoff run down the lake.

On the way back, he asked Jackson, "How in the world are they going to fix that thing? I know Tignak probably drove a tractor during the war, but Charlie's never even seen one."

Jackson grinned. "Prepare to be amazed," he said. "They will take it apart and figure out how it works. Then they'll put it together again, and it will run fine. Eskimos have wonderful minds. I always feel safer when an Eskimo mechanic works on my plane."

The return flight was pleasantly uneventful, and when Steve walked into the cabin, Liz met him with a beaming face. Sarah was there too, reading at the table. "Did everything go okay?"

"Just fine." He started to tell her about the trip, then stopped with a grin. "You're sure doing a lot of smiling. What's going on?"

"Sarah and I have been planning the Story Club, and she just told me the most wonderful news."

The girl looked up at him with a shy smile.

"Sarah, will you share your news with Mr. Steve?" said Liz.

Sarah kept a finger in her book to mark the place and stood up to face Steve. She gave him a quick glance from under her long black bangs, holding the book tightly against her. "You gone in summer, but I talk to my grandmother about God. Because all the time I am afraid. She ask me to read to her in Eskimo. That book of Mark. You know? Then she tell me how to pray."

Sarah's tan cheeks flushed pink, and her words came more quickly. "I talk to Jesus Christ. I thank Him for take the punishment of my sins. Now I belong to Him, and He take care of me."

"Sarah, what great news! I'm glad for you!"

So this was Sarah's secret. No wonder Tignak had looked so happy.

Liz put an arm around the girl and hugged her. "Sarah helped with the Story Club last year, but now she can help me teach too. We're both excited about it."

Sarah smiled and sat down again with her book. It was one of Liz's books, Steve noticed.

The next morning after the church service, Steve said to Liz, "Well, I'm glad the Lord gave us that encouraging news about Sarah yesterday. He knew what it would be like this morning."

Liz nodded. "It was difficult without Tignak, wasn't it? And I guess people knew he'd be away so they didn't come."

"But Victor's uncle was there," said Steve. "And Henry." He set his Bible and the Eskimo Gospel of Mark down on his desk. "This morning I was reminded again that we're involved in a spiritual warfare. I look at men like Victor and his uncle and Henry, and my heart aches because they're living in such fear. Charlie, too, with his amulets! And remember what Sarah said about being afraid?"

Liz nodded. "I sense it in the women too."

"Satan doesn't want us telling them about Christ, so we can expect a fight from him." He gazed out the window at the quiet log cabins. "Koyalik is our home base, but we've got opposition here. Mack is definitely not on our side. And from what I can tell, Shanaluk is shaping up as another battleground."

"And Mierow Lake?"

"Yes, Mierow Lake. Peter discovered that little village just a week before his plane crashed." He took a deep breath. "I wonder whether that plane crash was supposed to stop him from going back to preach the gospel."

"Well, we're going back!" exclaimed Liz. "Tomorrow! I'm all ready and I can't wait to see them!"

# 4 Samson of Mierow Lake

They left on Monday afternoon, under blue skies that glittered with fall sunlight. Once again, Steve set a course north by northeast and filed a flight plan.

He followed the branch of the Tiskleet that Jackson had pointed out. It twisted north across the tundra and led them to the foothills of the mountains. In less than an hour they were flying over valleys of dark green spruce brightened by glistening streams. Faint trails, probably made by caribou, crossed the ridges and meandered along the riverbanks.

He glanced into the back seat. Mikki, restrained by a cargo net, was curled up, asleep.

The mountain peak that Jackson called Old Man's Hat rose ahead of them, and Steve adjusted his course slightly to the east.

It was only a few months ago—last spring—that he and Jackson had flown to Mierow Lake in Jackson's Piper Cub. On that trip, Steve had left the people in the village with dozens of Eskimo Gospels of Mark. Jacob Nanouk had promised to use the booklets for a Bible study in his home.

What had happened since then?

Liz must have been thinking ahead too. "I wonder how the Nanouks have been doing. And Samson. I always liked him. There's something steady and deep in those black eyes of his."

"I hope Samson's been going to Nanouk's Bible studies," said Steve. "Remember how he wanted me to give him prayers to memorize? If he could get to know Christ for himself, he wouldn't feel like he needed that."

They flew down a long valley, and a crescent-shaped lake appeared below his left wing. Good. That's how he'd remembered Mierow Lake from his trip with Jackson. Steep mountains rose on all sides, and he planned his approach carefully. At least the lake was plenty long.

The whole trip had taken less than two hours: two comfortable hours, compared to two days of long, cold hours by dogsled.

From the back seat, Mikki whined softly; then he yawned a huge, noisy yawn. Liz reached back to pat him.

"Almost there, boy," Steve said, beginning his descent.

Jacob Nanouk stood at the edge of the water, and he was the first to shake Steve's hand. He talked nonstop, his face glowing, while Steve tied the airplane to a sturdy tree at the water's edge.

Dozens of people crowded forward to greet them, and once again the children admired Mikki. "Lookit wolf," they cried, as they had before. "Mister, do he bite?"

"No, he likes children," Steve said, and a few of them came close enough to pat Mikki and scratch behind his ears.

Steve saw Samson's beaming face in the crowd, but Jacob Nanouk was leading him into the village to show him the new buildings. Steve looked back to find Liz, and she waved him on. She and Mikki would stay with the Cessna. Good for her.

Nanouk pointed out their new general store, the one they had been building the last time Steve was there.

"And see this," the Eskimo exclaimed. He pointed to a long cabin in the middle of the village. The logs still had the honey color of freshly peeled logs, so it must have been built recently. "Our church!"

Nanouk took Steve inside to show him a narrow room, rather dark, that was filled with rows of benches. At the front was a platform for the speaker, and on the back wall, a gigantic cross painted bright red.

Steve gazed at it in surprise.

Nanouk answered his unspoken question. "We see in book. Good idea for our church too."

He ushered Steve outside and turned farther into the village. "Look my new house."

"Let's get my wife," said Steve. "I would like her to come too."

"Oh yes, she can talk to Mary," said Nanouk.

They returned to the plane and found Samson helping Liz to unload it and carry supplies into their cabin.

While Steve talked to Nanouk about having meetings during the week, he watched Samson filling the water barrel and stacking wood outside their cabin door.

Liz came over to join them, and Nanouk shook her hand with enthusiasm. "You will come to eat with us now, yes?"

"Well, thank you," she said. "We'd like that very much. I'll be ready in just a minute."

She hurried off to thank Samson for his help, and Steve chained Mikki to his usual place outside the cabin. Mikki would let the whole world know if anyone went near the cabin or the plane.

Nanouk's new cabin was the largest in the village, and it boasted such modern items as an oil stove for cooking and a plastic table with chairs to match.

"That Formica table looks like Victor's," Liz whispered to Steve. "It must have come from the same catalog."

Mary Nanouk was shy, but she quickly served up a meal of beaver stew. Nanouk prayed over the food, a short prayer that he said very fast.

The stew was thick and dark, and Steve ate it slowly, savoring its rich flavor. After Nanouk had finished his first bowl of stew, he put down his spoon and told them that the church had grown large during the past few months. He interrupted himself by banging a hand to his forehead. "I have something important to ask, and I forget until just now."

Steve waited expectantly as Nanouk paused. Maybe a question had come up in Bible study that he wanted to have explained.

"In airplane do you see caribou? We wait and wait for them to come. But you can see down from airplane and find them." Nanouk looked hopeful.

"I didn't notice any herds, but I did see some trails."

"Good, good. Okay, you finished eating, you give me little ride in plane and we find caribou?" In his excitement, Nanouk's English became more ragged. "For people hungry."

"Well, sure, I guess we could do that," said Steve. "But it's getting dark. How about tomorrow?"

He and Nanouk agreed to make a flight the next morning, and Nanouk promised that he'd arrange a meeting for that very night.

The little church was almost full when Steve began the service. Liz was sitting near the front, and she caught his eye with a smile. She'd be praying for him. The people remembered the songs he had taught them, and they sang loudly. Light from dozens of lanterns shone on the earnest, dark faces, and Steve prayed again that God would speak to their hearts through him.

He preached in English, since most of them understood it, and everyone listened intently. He told how God had answered their prayers for an airplane and emphasized God's faithfulness in supplying the needs of His people. He referred to the need for meat in their village. "My wife and I are praying that God will help you to find caribou," he said. His audience nodded and smiled with approval.

Later, back at the cabin, he and Liz talked about the service. "I wonder where those Gospels of Mark went," she said. "Didn't you leave some here?"

"Yes," said Steve, "but I didn't see anybody carrying one tonight. I'll have to ask Nanouk."

"Samson had one."

"Good for him! Maybe he'll know what happened to the rest of them."

The next morning, Nanouk arrived at their door in the gray light of dawn. An early morning fog still lay across the lake, but they took off without problems and soon were flying over the mountains that surrounded Mierow Lake.

They crossed a ridge and descended into the next valley, and suddenly Nanouk shouted, "*Araha, tutu!* (Look, caribou!)"

Steve banked the plane steeply to give Nanouk a better view of the herd below. The plane tilted sideways until it stood on one wing, and Nanouk gasped and drew back from the window. "Okay. Okay, I see plenty caribou. Good we go back now."

As soon as they landed, Nanouk struggled out of the plane, exclaiming, "I go get hunters!"

"When will you come back?" Steve called after him.

"One day, maybe two." Nanouk beamed in anticipation of a good hunt. No doubt, all the men of the village would go with him.

Steve shook his head and wandered back to the cabin to tell Liz what happened.

"What are you going to do now?" she asked.

"I've been meaning to give the Cessna a coat of wax so the paint would last longer. Might as well start on that." He splashed out to where the plane was moored and got a rag and can of wax from the baggage compartment. As he worked, he prayed, "Lord, I know You have a plan for this trip. Show us why You brought us here."

He had waxed all the way down one side of the plane's fuselage when he heard Mikki, still on shore, give a yip of greeting. Steve glanced across the water. A tall Eskimo was standing outside the cabin, talking to Liz.

Samson?

Hurriedly he closed the can of wax and waded to shore. "You're still here?"

"Plenty of hunters to go with Nanouk," Samson said. "A few men stay here, and the women. Do you have time to talk to us?"

Steve almost dropped the can of wax. "Do I? Sure."

Liz's eyes were shining. "Samson, I'd like to get together with the women. They can bring their kids. Could you tell them? We'll have a good time."

A smile glimmered across Samson's weather-beaten face. "Okay. I get them."

Liz gathered the women and children into the church, and after Steve had helped to rearrange the benches, he went with Samson and three other men to Samson's cabin. Each man carried a tattered black booklet—a Gospel of Mark—and when Steve saw that, he felt like singing.

He learned that Nanouk hadn't done much about having a Bible study, but this small group had been meeting with Samson ever since his last visit. They had read through the whole Gospel of Mark and had plenty of questions. Before they began, Samson prayed aloud. "Lord, please make light in our hearts so we understand Your Word. Give us ears like fox to hear what You say."

That certainly wasn't a memorized prayer, Steve thought. I wish Peter were here. He'd love to be part of this.

The time went so quickly that he was surprised when Liz came to the door in the middle of the afternoon.

"Aren't you guys hungry?" she asked. "C'mon, we've got food ready."

The hunters returned late that night with the carcasses of two caribou, having left several more cached on the other side of the mountain.

The next day, the whole village was busy. The women used their sharp *ulus* to cut up the animals, and nothing went to waste. The back fat was carefully removed to use in cooking. The sinews were separated and set aside to dry. They would serve as strong thread. The skins, carefully tanned, would become winter clothes—pants, socks, gloves, parkas—and the heavy bull skins could be made into mattresses.

By sundown, the butchering was finished. Steve began to hope for a meeting, but now the village had to have a feast. Nanouk invited Steve and Liz to his cabin for a meal of fresh caribou and honored Steve by presenting him with a steaming piece of boiled caribou heart.

Between mouthfuls of steak, Nanouk described how he had led the hunters over the mountain to the ridge where he had seen caribou from the airplane. "Then we wait," he said, "then they come, and I shoot first. Bang! Bang! My gun does not miss. I shoot again and again. Every time I hit one, and it fall down."

He paused to drain his cup of tea and help himself to another steak. Steve tried to steer the conversation around to the church. "You have a fine church building," he said.

"Who preaches there? Have you had a chance to read the Gospels of Mark together?"

Nanouk sat up straight. "I talk to the people. Not use Mark books very much, but almost everyone belong to church. Look here." He hoisted himself to his feet and brought a red notebook to the table. "Here are rules of church." The first pages had numbered sentences written in Eskimo.

Nanouk flipped to a list of names at the back of the book. "Here are names—all people who want to be in church promise to keep rules."

"Rules? What rules?"

"You know: no drinking, no smoking, be nice to wife and children, learn prayers." Nanouk looked thoughtful. "Keep rules and join church, then go to heaven."

Steve put down his fork. "Who told you that you have to keep rules to go to heaven?"

"This summer, old, old man missionary come talk to us. He go away, but we remember. Rules make God happy. And you tell us about God too. We want Steve happy. We want God happy. So we try to keep rules."

Steve almost choked trying to swallow the piece of caribou he had been chewing on. Finally he said, "I can stay only two more days. May I talk to the church tomorrow and Friday? And could you please ask anyone who has a Gospel of Mark to bring it along?"

Nanouk smiled in agreement. "Yes, yes, meetings. Bring books. Tomorrow afternoon and tomorrow night meetings. And Friday in the morning. Then we get ready for feast."

"Another feast?"

"Yes." Nanouk proudly surveyed the crowded cabin. "My son, he have his first birthday on Friday."

That night Steve and Liz prayed together for Nanouk and Samson and his small Bible study group. Then, for a long time after Liz had fallen asleep, Steve talked to the Lord about what he should preach.

For all three meetings, he spoke from the second chapter of Mark, concentrating on the story of how Christ had forgiven the sins of a sick man and then had healed him.

"I have seen your book of rules," Steve said. "Those are good rules, but they can't take away sins. This man did not keep rules in order to have his sins forgiven. He couldn't even get out of bed. He came to Christ the way he was— weak and sick and helpless."

He had asked Samson to read the Bible passage aloud in Eskimo at the beginning of each meeting. Each time the tall Eskimo stood up to read, the people grew quiet.

But while Steve was preaching, there seemed to be endless distractions. Babies cried, and no one hushed them. Children scampered up and down the aisle. Dogs ran in and out. People smiled and whispered to each other.

At the final meeting, Friday morning, Samson finished the Bible reading and then spoke directly to the people. Steve couldn't follow the complicated Eskimo sentences, but this time it seemed that the people listened to his preaching more carefully than before.

That afternoon, when Steve met with the Bible study group at Samson's house, he asked the tall Eskimo what he had said to the people.

Samson's black eyes gleamed. "I tell them we sick like that man when we don't know Christ. Our sin make us sick, and God is angry about that. We can't make God happy by keeping rules. But if we come to Him through Christ, He forgive our sins and let us come into His heaven."

"Good for you!" said Steve. "That's exactly right."

When he came back from Samson's house, Liz said, "Well, you sure preached your heart out in those meetings. I hope they heard you in spite of everything that was going on."

"I hope so too. Afterward, everyone was so polite and kind. Eskimos are nice that way. But Samson told them some good things. I talked to him, and I'm sure he's a believer. He's having a great ministry with his little group."

"I'm glad for that." Liz glanced at her watch. "Oh! I promised to go help Mary."

"Remember those Bibles Peter sent us?" asked Steve. "Don't you think Samson should get one?"

"Yes!" exclaimed Liz. "We can bring it the next time we come. Peter will be thrilled!" She smiled and reached for her parka. "I'll see you later, then. It sounds as if the food is going to be interesting tonight."

The feast was as happy and noisy as most Eskimo celebrations, and Steve listened carefully to the songs and hunting stories, trying to absorb the culture.

Many gifts were brought to the youngest son of Jacob Nanouk. Among them were a tiny pair of embroidered mukluks, a soft ball made of tanned caribou skin, and a carved wooden rattle with pebbles inside.

The last gift was wrapped in a piece of black wolf fur that glistened richly in the lantern light. Mary's face glowed when she saw what it was. "Ah . . . ah . . . !" she exclaimed in admiration.

She held up a gleaming string of pointed white teeth. "Teeth from wolf!" she cried. "My son, he will be strong and courageous, a mighty hunter!" Then she continued in Eskimo, saying something about the soul of the wolf.

Steve exchanged a look with Liz and groaned to himself.

That night, he lay awake for a long time in the dark cabin, listening to the rustling noises on the floor behind the stove. Mierow Lake was definitely going to be a battleground, even though so many of the people claimed to be Christians. They were hung up on following rules, and they couldn't seem to let go of their superstitions. This might be harder to deal with than an angry shaman.

Tonight after they'd returned from the feast, he and Liz had talked and prayed over the problems in the church. Their psalm to read together had been Psalm 18, and in the middle of the psalm were verses about war that caught Steve's attention. Now he remembered some fragments: *He teacheth my hands to war . . . Thou hast girded me with strength unto the battle. . . .*

He rolled over in his sleeping bag, and a small creature skittered away in the darkness. Yes, the ministry here would be a battle. So far, God had given them only one believer, Samson. "Lord," he whispered, "he's in this warfare with us. Make him strong for whatever comes."

A twinge of pain shot through his jaw. What was that for? He covered it with one hand to keep off the cold air, and while he was still warming it, he fell asleep.

The next day they took off under cloudy skies. All the way to Koyalik, while the Cessna jiggled and bounced in the rough air, Steve thought about the young church they had left behind. He rubbed at his jaw, which was aching again.

Liz looked a little downcast, and her face grew whiter every time the plane lurched. She was probably airsick on top of everything else.

A verse jerked into his mind, the verse from the book of Joshua that had encouraged them ever since they'd come to Koyalik. He said it aloud, raising his voice above the thunder of the engine. *"Have not I commanded thee? Be strong and of a good courage; be not afraid, neither be thou dismayed: for the Lord thy God is with thee—"*

Liz joined in as he finished it: *"—whithersoever thou goest."*

# 5 I Fix Tooth

Liz struggled through the heavy cabin door, her arms full of clothes she had taken from the line outside. "These shirts of yours are about frozen stiff, you know. It's getting cold."

She dropped the clothes onto the table and hung two of Steve's shirts over the rope that ran down the center of the cabin. "They'll have to dry in here for awhile, but at least you'll have a clean shirt for church tomorrow."

She shivered. "It's probably even colder for Tignak and Charlie, wherever they are. When do you think they'll get back? If they don't hurry, it'll be freeze-up and we'll start having those blizzards."

Steve looked up from the letter he was reading. "They've only been gone for a week. We've got to allow them at least a week to fix the tractor and another week or two to drive the thing down here. No roads, remember."

"Sorry," said Liz. "We've been praying for them so much, and they're always on my mind. I just can't wait for them to get here."

"I know. And I can't wait to talk to Tignak about Mierow Lake. Maybe he could go back there with me. Imagine—the child of a so-called Christian wearing a wolf amulet. And keeping all those rules to make God happy."

"I guess they figure it's safer to stay with the old taboos. And they probably think of the rules as sort of Christian taboos."

"I'm afraid so," said Steve. He rubbed at his jaw. "I wonder whether I've got a toothache."

Liz looked up from the clothes she was folding. "A toothache? And there's no dentist around here anywhere. I'll make you a cup of peppermint tea. Maybe that'll help."

While she made his tea, Steve re-read the letters that had come in when they were at Mierow Lake. "This is sure a great letter from Peter," he said. "I'm glad we had a chance to visit him when we were in the States. That guy is always so encouraging—and he's the one stuck in a wheelchair. Talk about a prayer warrior! I've got to write and tell him what's happening in Mierow Lake."

He shuffled the envelopes into a pile and opened his notebook to work on tomorrow's message. "When I picked up the mail, Gus told me that Nida and the kids are coming back on Monday's mail plane."

Liz put a steaming mug at his elbow. "How'd he find out?"

"I think everyone tells Gus what's going on. He's better than a newspaper."

"I'll go see Nida when they get here. Maybe they can come for supper."

The meal on Monday night, with Nida, her three small boys, Sarah, and the grandmother, was lively and noisy. Mikki received a great deal of attention from the children and didn't seem to mind when the baby crawled across his back and pulled at his tail.

Nida's pretty young face looked drawn, Steve thought, and her laugh sounded brittle. She did not mention Victor, but Steve knew he was still upriver at the fish camp. Gus said that he had come down briefly to buy supplies at the Trading Post and left right away.

Steve thought about Victor. What could he do to help his friend? Should he try going up to see him? The women were talking about the Story Club and making plans for the coming week. Cutting up salmon and picking berries, it sounded like. He rubbed at the pain in his jaw.

Nida must have noticed, for she turned to him. "You have sore tooth?"

"I guess so. It's been sort of bothering me for a couple of days."

She nodded, and a smile lightened her somber face. "I fix. Tomorrow I bring you medicine; then Liz and I go pick berries."

Sure enough, the next morning while Steve and Liz were still finishing breakfast, Nida appeared at the door. "This for berries." She handed Liz a small wooden pail that was bound with thongs of rawhide.

She carried a similar pail, as did her two young sons. The baby rode on her back, inside her parka, and he waved and called to Mikki.

"Oh, good! I'll be ready in a minute," said Liz. "Sit down and have some tea."

Nida took a small bottle from her pocket and set it on the table. "I fix tooth now," she said to Steve. She pulled out a ptarmigan feather. "Open mouth. Where it hurt?"

Steve didn't see any way to refuse, so he obeyed. Nida dipped the feather into the bottle and smeared his gum with a dark liquid.

Instantly his mouth was on fire. He jerked away.

She smiled placidly. "Little bit hurt now. Then feel better." She turned to Liz. "Okay for berries?"

"Ready." They went outside, already laughing and talking.

Steve spat the awful-tasting stuff into the sink, snatched up his axe, and went out to chop wood. Maybe that would take his mind off the raging pain in his mouth. He took a deep breath of the crisp air and winced as the cold hit his tooth. So much for ancient Eskimo remedies.

While he was chopping wood, one person after another stopped to talk to him, and by the time the wood box was full, he realized that he hadn't thought about his tooth for quite a while. It didn't seem to be hurting anymore either.

The next day when Steve went up to the Trading Post, he told the old trader about Nida's toothache remedy. "I wonder what was in it," he said. "It sure took care of my tooth."

"Sit down and have some coffee," Gus said. His broad face wrinkled with amusement. "She painted the stuff on with a feather, right?"

"Right."

"I hope you didn't swallow any of it."

"No. I had to spit it out. It tasted terrible. And it hurt like crazy."

"Yah, I know. They all use it, and I've never figured out why it works. Or why they aren't all dead. That stuff was iodine."

"Iodine? That's poison!"

"Certainly it is. But you'll probably be okay now for a couple of months. Maybe sometime you can get to a dentist in Nome." Gus poured himself another cup of coffee and asked, "Did Nida hear from Victor yet?"

"No. When do you think he'll come back?"

"Probably when the river freezes over. I need to talk to that boy."

Steve stirred more sugar into his coffee. It might be soon then. Already the weather had turned colder. Fewer ducks swam on the lagoon, and the cries of wild geese rang through the sky.

"I want to talk to Victor too," he said. But what could he say that Victor hadn't already heard?

As he walked back to his cabin, he prayed again for Victor. One thing he could do was to bring Peter up to date about Victor so he could pray too. Peter had made friends with the young Eskimo when he first came to Koyalik as a missionary, and Victor had been kind enough to translate Peter's messages each Sunday.

Come to think of it, what were they going to do this Sunday? He couldn't preach well enough in Eskimo to make sense. Victor was upriver, and Tignak was still away.

What about Henry? The sturdy young Eskimo knew some English, and he seemed more and more interested in what was going on. Maybe he could be persuaded to translate.

The next day around noon, Steve and Liz walked over to Henry's cabin. He was working on the outboard motor for his boat, but he politely took them inside.

His wife, Emma, put down the net she was mending and jumped to her feet. "Hello, hello!" she said, her round face beaming. "Stay for lunch." She stirred something in a skillet on the stove, and Liz went to join her.

A thin old man was sitting cross-legged on the floor by the stove, working intently with a knife. A bloody carcass lay beside him. Fur, blood, gristle, and bones were spread over the floor. He looked up, nodded, and went back to work.

"My father," said Henry. "He skin fox." While they talked, Henry's father worked silently, his head bowed in concentration.

The smell of frying meat filled the small cabin, and a few minutes later, Emma said, "Come and eat!" Henry's father put down his knife, wiped his hands on his pants, and sat down with them at the table.

Emma had set out fried seal liver, salmon, wild celery greens, fresh bread, and blueberries. As they ate and talked, Steve learned that Henry was reading his way through the Gospel of Mark on his own.

Henry knew where Tignak and Charlie had gone—everyone in the village knew that—and he agreed right away to help with the church service.

On the way back to their cabin, Steve heard from Liz about her conversation with Emma. "She's a marvelous cook, and such fun!" said Liz. "Oh, I found out that on Monday Henry's mother is coming back from a shopping trip to Nome."

"Okay," said Steve, "let's meet the mail plane. I want to get to know this family better."

# 6 To Am-nok

Monday, the mail plane didn't arrive until late afternoon; but everyone could hear it coming, so Steve and Liz and a dozen others were down at the airstrip when it landed. Mack was the pilot on this trip, and he let Henry's mother crawl stiffly out of the plane without giving the old woman a helping hand.

Mack was silent, briskly unloading the cargo, until Henry's father wandered over to look at the stall warning horn on the wing.

Mack's head snapped up. "Keep your hands to yourself," he said. "You're not getting any lights off my plane."

The old man backed away, his face impassive, but Henry spoke up. "That my father," he said with dignity. "You can trust him. He not steal your lights."

Mack straightened himself to his six-foot height and looked down at Henry. "Yeah. The only way I'll trust any of you is when I can keep an eye on every move you make."

Steve had picked up the old woman's suitcase, but now he put it down. "You making an accusation, Mack?"

"Stay out of this." The pilot took a step toward him, but Steve held his ground. He wasn't as heavy as Mack, but he was younger. If the pilot took a swing at him, he could always duck.

Steve looked squarely into the pilot's sunglasses. "These are my friends. Leave them alone."

"Friends!" The pilot spat out the word with contempt; then he shrugged, as if Steve were not worth bothering about. He turned back to the cargo, and after a while the silent crowd dispersed.

Liz spent the rest of the afternoon visiting Emma, and that evening she described for Steve what she had learned about tanning a fox pelt. "Oh, and I found out something. Henry's mother said that someone from Shanaluk told her the shaman is much worse these days."

"That's sad news," said Steve. "I keep hoping that Am-nok will change his mind. Maybe if he hears about Christ one more time. . . . I've got to go see him. I wanted to take Tignak with me, but I'd better not wait for him to get back." He thought for a minute. "Maybe Henry would go."

"Take Mikki too," said Liz.

"Okay. He likes to fly." Steve began lacing up his boots.

"We'll pray for you."

"We?"

"Yes, Sarah and I and Grandmother pray together every day. We have quite a few people on our list."

Henry agreed to go, and they left the next morning. Light rain fell from clouds that were high enough for Steve to fly under, but the air was a little rough. Henry had flown with Steve the previous year on an emergency flight to Nome, and today he was as calm as ever. A good kind of passenger to have, Steve thought.

Once they had landed at Shanaluk, they left Mikki to guard the airplane and walked slowly down a muddy lane to Am-nok's cabin. At the door, they shuffled their feet to make the correct amount of noise, then pushed it open. It still seemed strange to walk inside without knocking.

An old woman rose from beside the stove and silently inclined her head, as if she knew why they had come. Her face was dried and withered, as expressionless as a piece of wrinkled leather.

*She has no hope,* thought Steve. *No hope for this life or the next.* He wanted to put an arm around her thin shoulders and tell her about Christ, but he knew she wouldn't understand his broken Eskimo. He leaned toward her, and she turned away.

Rain pattered on the roof and drizzled against the window. It was dusk inside the cabin, and the smell of rancid seal oil and old, unwashed bodies hung in the air. A heaviness fell upon Steve, as if the powers of darkness had gathered there to do battle with him.

Am-nok lay on a cot under caribou skins and thick wolf pelts. His face was no longer plump; it was thin and lined with pain. His eyes were still unreadable, mere slits in the gaunt face.

Henry spoke first, and then Steve leaned close and said the Eskimo sentences he had practiced.

The man blinked, but he did not move. His breath came in short, shallow wheezes.

Steve opened his Gospel of Mark to the second chapter and handed it to Henry, who read aloud the story of Christ forgiving the sick man's sin. As Henry read, Steve prayed silently for the old shaman.

The wrinkled brown hand stirred, moving aimlessly in the rich wolf furs. Steve covered it with his own and prayed aloud in Eskimo and then in English, asking God to have mercy on Am-nok. In case the man could understand, he spoke of Christ's death on his behalf and told him how to receive the gift of eternal life.

He gazed into the dark eyes, and for an instant, they opened wide. The old man raised his hand feebly, then let it fall. Steve leaned forward, but Am-nok slowly turned his head away.

Behind them, the old woman rose from where she sat by the stove. She opened the door, as if to suggest that they should go, and they walked outside. Steve glanced at Henry and saw his own sadness mirrored in the young Eskimo's face.

Rain fell more steadily now, and the air was colder. Steve did not want to leave, but if they didn't hurry, fog would close down, and they wouldn't be able to get into Koyalik.

On the way back, he flew low over the river, avoiding a mass of clouds that were spitting snow. But even while he was watching the river and the clouds, part of his mind remained at Shanaluk, and he prayed once again for the dying shaman.

Beside him, Henry sat quietly, as usual. What was the young Eskimo thinking?

*Lord, speak to Henry too,* Steve prayed. *Use what he has seen and heard today to open his eyes to the truth.*

That evening, the clouds parted and gave way to stars, a full moon, and complete stillness. All night, wild geese flew south through the moonlight. Shimmering purple and pink streamers danced across the sky in the brightest display of the Northern Lights so far this season.

Next morning, the lagoon had frozen, and ice crystals frosted the pier with white and glittered at the river's edge.

"Freeze-up!" exclaimed Liz.

Steve thought first about his plane. "The river will be full of slush, so it's time to put on the skis. Jackson said he'd help me."

He wouldn't be able to fly now until the river ice hardened, but there was plenty to do in the village, and soon Tignak and Charlie would return. Each evening when Steve and Liz prayed together, one of them inevitably said, "I wonder how Tignak and Charlie did today." Liz always added, "I hope they're not too cold." And they prayed for God's protection on the two.

"You know," Steve said one evening, "this has probably been a good experience for Charlie."

"What do you mean?"

"He'll be seeing his father in action, and Tignak has been a different man since he believed in Christ. I hope Charlie notices that."

What was it going to take for the boy to see his own need of Christ?

At the end of the week, Liz and Steve were strolling back from the Trading Post when a small Eskimo boy ran down the lane, shouting.

"What's he saying, Steve?"

"Somebody's coming!" Steve grinned at her. "Maybe it's Tignak and Charlie. Let's go see."

They hurried to the edge of the village and stared to the east. A cloud of dust rumbled slowly toward them across the tundra.

"It is!" exclaimed Liz. "It's Tignak! Where's Charlie?"

The cloud of dust moved closer, and the sound of a roaring engine grew louder. A yellow tractor bumped over the hummocks of the tundra, pulling a heavily loaded sled. On top of the pile, holding onto the ropes with one hand and waving like a hero, sat Charlie.

"Amazing!" Steve had to shout over the deafening noise. "Just like Jackson said—amazing! I wonder if Tignak wishes there were a road into Koyalik right about now?"

The tractor stopped in front of Tignak's cabin and shuddered into silence. The whole village gathered around to welcome the pair and exclaim over this huge machine with its levers and switches and dials.

Tignak and Charlie headed straight through the crowd to Liz and Steve. Liz hugged them both in turn, and when Charlie stooped to put his arms around Mikki, the dog covered his face with wet kisses.

Tignak shook Steve's hand vigorously. "Thank you for praying."

"Supper at our house," said Liz. "Whenever you're ready."

The meal was silent at first. The food wasn't anything fancy—cabbage, rice, and salmon, something Liz called Russian pie—but Charlie and Tignak ate heartily. Charlie paused once to say, "My fadder not cook like you, Missus Lizzie." He grinned at his little sister. "Good you teach Sarah." Then he bent over his plate again.

Tignak only smiled and reached for another biscuit and the small pot of honey.

Over hot tea and dried apple pie, Charlie began to talk. "First, tractor don't start. Then it don't drive right. Then it go too slow."

The trip back had been interrupted time after time while they'd searched for a way to get across the many streams. Sometimes they had stopped to cut down trees and build a rough bridge of logs. One day Charlie shot a caribou, and then they had built a sled out of logs to carry the meat and their gear.

Tignak had decided to take a detour by way of Shanaluk and pick up some things from their old house.

"I went to see Am-nok," Tignak said. "Joseph told me you had been there."

"How is he now?" asked Steve.

Charlie stood up abruptly, as if he couldn't bear to hear what Tignak was going to say. He went to where Mikki lay by the door and crouched beside the dog.

Tignak shook his head. "Am-nok is pretty far gone. I spoke to him, but I don't know if he heard. The people say he has flown to the moon and is doing battle with another shaman. But I think he's fighting another kind of battle. If he heard me—if he heard you, Steve—perhaps we will see him in heaven."

Looking weary, Tignak got to his feet. "Liz, thank you very much for your kindness and for this good food." He handed Sarah her parka and pulled on his own. "Steve, I've been thinking about the church here, as you asked. I have a few ideas. Maybe we can talk tomorrow."

Victor returned the next day. Steve ran into him at the Trading Post and they had a long talk, Eskimo fashion, about the weather and this year's fishing. He took Victor down to the river and showed him the Cessna. Steve and Jackson had replaced the floats with skis, and the ice was now hard enough to land on. When the deep snow came, he would use the airstrip.

Victor's eyes didn't sparkle the way they used to, but he was as friendly as ever.

"Peter cover engine every night and warm up plane before he fly," he said, a remembering look on his face.

"Yes, I do too, now that it's so cold," said Steve. "I have a little stove for preheating the engine."

"And you take out battery and oil?" Victor chuckled. "Nida always think it so funny to keep oil warm on Peter's stove."

Steve smiled at that. "Yes, Liz thinks it's pretty strange too, but it's worth it to keep the plane flying."

When Liz heard that Victor was back, she said, "I'm going to invite them for supper. Maybe things will be better now that Elsa Danner isn't here anymore."

"From what Gus said, Victor might be doing some serious thinking about his drinking problem," said Steve. "Gus sat him down and told him some horror stories about how liquor has destroyed a lot of Eskimo families."

Nida and Victor agreed to come for supper. Victor seemed glad to be there, and Nida was more like her bright, cheerful self. They stayed late, talking about the new airplane and about Liz and Steve's experiences during the summer. Afterward, Steve decided that the evening together had been a start toward a renewed friendship.

Tuesday morning, Steve was eating breakfast when a young Eskimo appeared at his door. "Gus say come quick!"

Steve hurried into his clothes and followed the boy out into the dark, icy morning. The wind that had set in yesterday scraped his face, and he could hear it blowing across the pack ice.

Nida was lying on the couch in Gus's apartment. She clutched at her stomach, moaning. Victor knelt beside her.

Gus's hair stood up in unruly clumps around the bald spot on his head. "That idiot pilot we've got—what's he mean he *doesn't have time*—and did he ever come back? No! So what do we have? She's got appendicitis, and I've done plenty of doctoring, but I'm not about to try surgery when there's a perfectly good hospital in Nome—"

Steve put a hand on the old trader's arm. "What's going on, Gus? Why didn't Mack want to fly her to Nome?"

"He had to deliver something—somewhere—and he was running late and he thought a storm was coming in. You know what Jackson would have done?"

Steve nodded. Jackson would have taken her straight to Nome, never mind the delivery or the storm.

He looked down at Nida. "How bad is she?"

"Bad as I've ever seen. High fever. She's got to get there soon or . . ."

Victor jerked toward them. His eyes burned with pain and with something else. Guilt?

"Yah, that storm's coming," said Gus. "Can you take her?"

# 7 Weapons of War

Steve glanced at Gus's radio. "What's the forecast?"

"A front moving in; they're expecting heavy snow."

"When?"

"It sounds like you'll run into it before you get to Nome."

Not so good. But he couldn't let Nida die.

He scraped at the frost on the window and peered through the small opening. A few stars were still up there. The sun wouldn't rise for another hour or two. *Lord, please give me Your wisdom.*

He swung around to face them. "Okay. I'll start preheating the engine. Victor, you go tell Liz what's happening. Get the battery from her and the bucket of oil. Tell her I'll need coffee and some extra clothes in case I get stuck in Nome for a few days. It's a good thing we've got the survival gear already onboard. Oh, and ask Charlie if he'll come help me with the plane."

He stopped to think, wishing it were daylight. "It's too dark to take off unless I can see down the river. Gus, can you get some men ready with lanterns—maybe six? Show them where to stand on the river; you know, like runway lights. Okay, let's see how fast we can get out of here."

The wind was still light, but it seemed to intensify the cold, turning the breath in Steve's nostrils to ice. Charlie took care of the camp stove that was preheating the engine, and Steve and Victor removed the copilot's seat in order to replace it with a small stretcher that Gus kept for emergencies. It would go in lengthwise, with one end resting on the back seat.

Victor touched his arm. "Let me come."

Steve shook his head. "No way. You stay with those three little boys of yours. Here's what I'll do: Nome is too far away for direct radio contact, so I'll have to get a radio message relayed to Gus. But if the storm lets up after a couple of days and you haven't heard from me, that'll mean we didn't make it. Come look for us with the dogs. Use Mikki."

Victor gave him a worried glance, but he nodded and began loading the supplies Liz had brought. Steve beat his mittened hands together in the numbing cold and began his preflight check.

When Gus returned from organizing the men with lanterns, he helped Victor get Nida onboard. Steve made sure that she was securely tied onto the stretcher, then he strapped the stretcher into place with the seat belt and covered her with two extra blankets. "I'm sorry it's so cold in here," he said to her, "but it will warm up soon."

Nida managed to smile, and she murmured something he couldn't hear.

The wind began to rise, tugging at the Cessna's wings as Steve finished the preflight check. He gave Liz a quick hug, climbed into the cockpit, and started the engine.

Between the ragged clouds above, stars twinkled erratically. Blurred light on the horizon promised that dawn was near, but the river ice lay in darkness, lit only by the flickering lanterns.

After the engine was warmed, he taxied into position for takeoff. "Okay, Nida, hang on."

The Cessna swept down the ice between the pairs of lanterns and rose easily into the air. As they turned north, the dots of light below were swallowed up in darkness.

"Well, we're off." He said it confidently, as much for his benefit as for Nida's.

He filed a flight plan, trying to ignore the worry that nibbled at the edge of his mind. The most direct route to Nome was across Norton Sound, but he had heard too many stories about planes going down on the ice. Sometimes the pack ice broke away from the shelf ice, and the floes drifted toward the open sea. Weeks later, someone found the wreckage.

"I'm going to fly the coastline," he said to Nida. "Then there's a better chance of rescue . . ." He didn't say any more. If the plane went down, they most likely would not survive. In spite of all his precautions, one or both of them would probably die from the impact or from the cold.

The plane climbed smoothly to cruising altitude and hummed into the gray north.

After a while the sky lightened, but only enough to show that he was flying in a whiteout. "Like flying inside a bottle of milk," Jackson would say.

He stared below through thickening fog, looking for the cliffs he would follow up the coast, but all he could see was white.

Although Nida did not answer, he kept talking to her, trying to relax, to settle down and fly as if this were just another trip. "Actually, I've never flown in a whiteout before, but the Lord knows all about this. He'll take care of us." Was she listening? "Stick to your instruments, Jackson told me."

He scanned his instruments: the artificial horizon, the airspeed indicator, back to the artificial horizon, the altimeter, the artificial horizon again, the directional gyro. Okay.

The minutes ticked past. Ten minutes. Fifteen.

He tried not to look through the windshield because it showed only white. He tried to ignore the fact that he couldn't tell whether he was flying up, down, or sideways. The artificial horizon said he was flying straight and level, and the directional gyro confirmed that he was headed in the right direction. *Stick to your instruments.*

Finally, through a thin spot in the fog below, he glimpsed the buildings of a village and beyond it, the shelf ice. Good; he was still on course.

Half an hour passed before the fog lifted enough for him to see the cliffs along the coastline. "Hey, Nida, the fog seems to be clearing up a bit, and those cliffs are right where they're supposed to be. But now we're getting snow. Nome has got to be just ahead of us. I sure do wish I could talk to someone there. You doing okay?"

She did not answer, and he glanced at her. She was lying awfully still.

He kept talking. "Just look at this stuff!" Snow blew against the windshield and whirled past the windows, white into white.

Maybe now he was close enough to raise Nome on the radio. He tried it: "Nome radio, this is Cessna 1577 Zebra. Do you read?"

He turned up his receiver, and the harsh sound of static filled the cockpit.

Five long minutes later, he tried again. Still no answer.

He poured a cup of coffee from the thermos and was dismayed to see that his hands were shaking. "Lord, I need your strength," he whispered. The verse from Joshua filled his mind: *Have not I commanded thee? Be strong and of a good courage . . .* He gulped down the burning liquid and scanned his instruments once more.

The radio crackled. A faint voice said, "Cessna 1577 Zebra, do you read me?"

He snatched up the microphone. "Roger, this is 77 Zebra. I have a medical emergency onboard. I'd appreciate your help getting down, and I'll need an ambulance."

"Roger, 77 Zebra. Do you have the approach plates for Nome?"

"Affirmative."

"Okay, we'll be using the NDB range marker approach for runway two-seven."

"Roger, I've got it tuned in, but I can just barely pick it up at the moment."

Must be getting close. He still couldn't see anything beyond the swirling white, but at least he had radio contact. Good thing there weren't any trees or mountains around here.

The time stretched into another half hour; then the radio voice came back. "77 Zebra, I hear you. Sounds like you're overhead."

"Roger, my needle just told me I'd crossed the beacon."

"Roger, 77 Zebra, do a procedure turn, go outbound, and get set up on the inbound leg of the range marker. Altimeter setting is two-niner-six-two."

He followed the approach plates, descending through the snow to a lower altitude. "Okay," he muttered, "am I over the runway or over a hangar now? Where are those lights?"

At last he saw the approach lights glowing through the snow, and he breathed more easily. Now he could come down.

*Thunk*—his skis touched snow. A wonderful feeling.

Cautiously he taxied toward the dim outline of a building next to the runway. "Hang in there, Nida. Just a few minutes."

A man bundled in furs appeared through the curtain of snow and shouted something. Steve opened his window, letting in a flurry of white.

"You're out of your mind," the man yelled, "flying in this—"

"I've got a dying woman aboard. You got that ambulance?"

The man turned and ran back toward the hanger.

Steve unclipped the seat belt from the stretcher and took Nida's hand into his own. It was hot and dry. "C'mon girl, you can do it," he whispered.

Two men ran up with a long stretcher, eased Nida's small stretcher out of the airplane, and disappeared into the white gloom.

After the ambulance left, he tied down the Cessna with extra care, conscious of the tearing wind that snatched at the airplane's wings and tail, then lugged his duffle bag toward the lights of the hangar. He stood for a minute in its warmth and shook the snow out of his eyes. Then he borrowed their phone to call a taxi, wishing there was some way he could get in touch with Gus. But no one in Koyalik had a phone.

His taxi drove up through the blowing snow, and he was glad to get inside and let someone else handle the weather. In the few minutes it took to reach the hospital, he learned that the wiry little driver spent his summers working a gold mine in the hills behind Nome, that milk had gone up to sixty-five cents a quart, and that the storm would last for three days.

Nida was already in the operating room by the time he walked into the small hospital. He gave the nurse the information she wanted and sat down to wait in a big overstuffed chair.

He picked up a magazine and tried to read. It sure was nice and warm in here. When he closed his eyes, he could see the whirling snow and hear the Cessna's engine roaring in his ears.

A long while later, he jerked awake. A gray-headed doctor stood in front of him. "You the pilot who brought in Mrs. Norlik?"

"Yes, sir." Steve rubbed at his aching neck and struggled to stand up.

"Bad appendix. She's going to be okay. An hour more would have been too late." The doctor inclined his head. "Got us a blizzard out there. Good work."

"Thank you, sir." Steve hesitated. "She has a very anxious family back in Koyalik. Could I use your telephone to call the airport? Maybe I can get a message to them."

"Certainly." The doctor showed him to a desk with a telephone, and Steve phoned the airline office. They promised to send a radio message to Koyalik with the next plane going south, and he hung up, hoping a plane could get out of Nome tomorrow.

The nurse told him about a hotel just down the street, so he fought his way through the snow toward the dim lights of a tall square building and arranged for a room. He couldn't remember when he'd last eaten, but there was a small restaurant next door.

He ate two bowls of thick moose stew, then stumbled back to the hotel and up a flight of dark, narrow stairs to his room. Without bothering to change, he stretched out on the lumpy bed and instantly fell asleep.

He awoke with a confused sense of time having passed, but it wasn't until he looked at his watch that he realized it was mid-morning. Must have slept through the whole afternoon and night. He stepped to the window and peered through limp brown curtains. Nothing out there but white. Snowflakes still whirled into the ten-inch cap of fresh snow on the window ledge.

He stared into the blizzard. At least he wasn't trying to fly through it. What a mercy that the Lord had allowed them to get into Nome before the blizzard shut down the airport.

*Thank you, Lord!* He leaned against the window and prayed for Nida and for Victor, for Tignak, and especially for Charlie.

Cold seeped in around the scarred window frame, stirring the limp curtains and making him shiver. This storm was probably burying Koyalik too. He prayed for Liz, carrying on alone. Maybe she had taken Mikki into the cabin for company, as she often did. No planes would be flying today, and she'd be wondering what had happened to him.

Thinking about Liz reminded him of their verse in Joshua 1:9. The Book of Joshua had a lot of warfare in it, a lot about fighting the Lord's battles. He sat down on the bed and opened his Bible.

Joshua chapter one. He read the first few verses. Moses had died, and God had appointed Joshua as commander-in-chief. Joshua was to lead the armies of Israel into the land that God had promised them.

He turned on the small lamp by the bed and settled back against the pillow to read further. Again and again in the first seven verses, God told Joshua not to be afraid, that He would lead them to victory. In verse eight, God reminded Joshua that obeying His laws would bring him blessing.

Then, like a trumpet call to action, came the promise in verse nine:

*Have not I commanded thee?*
*Be strong and of a good courage;*
*be not afraid, neither be thou dismayed:*
*for the Lord thy God is with thee*
*whithersoever thou goest.*

He re-read the end of the verse: *whithersoever thou goest.* Joshua didn't know it yet, but in the days to come, God was going to lead him up and down the land of Canaan, fighting one battle after another. *Whithersoever.* An odd word, but a good way of saying "in every single place."

Like . . . Koyalik. Shanaluk. Mierow Lake. Nome.

He smiled to himself. He and Liz didn't have bows and arrows for fighting their battles, but God had given them the Cessna. And, even better, His Word! The Book of Ephesians spoke of Satan and spiritual warfare and "the sword of the Spirit, which is the Word of God." God had given them His promises, and for the Eskimo people, those wonderful Gospels of Mark.

He bowed his head over the open Bible. "Lord, make me strong for this warfare," he prayed. "Make me a good soldier, trusting You and obeying Your Word."

Slowly he closed his Bible and stood up. Outside, the snow still fell heavily, but he could see lights gleaming from a restaurant across the street. The storm seemed to have let up for a minute. First he'd get something to eat, and then he'd check on Nida and explore Nome.

# 8 The Walrus Hunt

"So you explored Nome," said Liz. "What did you find?"

"A fairly wide main street, about three blocks long, with a supermarket, a general store, a drugstore, and two hotels," said Steve. "A couple of restaurants too."

"Any houses?"

"As far as I could see, which wasn't far, they were mostly log cabins and tarpaper shacks. All buried in snow, of course. Looks like you got plenty here too."

"We sure did." Liz bent over his duffle bag, shaking out wrinkled clothes. "I'm so glad Tignak has that tractor. He used it to clear the runway, and then he plowed the lane that goes down to the Trading Post. What's this?"

She held up a small brown paper bag that looked as if someone had sat on it. Mikki rose from under the table and gave it a sniff.

"Oh, I brought you a cinnamon roll from the North Pole Bakery."

Liz pulled out a broken piece of roll and tasted it. "M-m-m—this is delicious!"

"They've got some wonderful stuff at that bakery. I'd like to take you there."

Liz smiled and fished out another piece of roll. "Sounds good to me! But maybe not today. Tignak's coming over for supper, and then he wants to talk about plans for tomorrow's Sunday service."

"You're right." Steve yawned widely. The Lord had given him clear weather and an easy flight back, but he was still tired. "How's Charlie been?"

"He's doing fine. A big help to me while you were gone. He shoveled out the path and kept me supplied with ice for the water barrel. He chopped plenty of wood. I think he's partial to chocolate-chip cookies."

"Well, I don't blame him!" Steve sat down to oil his rifle. "It sure does smell good in here. I'm glad to be home, I can tell you."

"For a while I wondered if you'd make it back. I started getting afraid." Liz got to her feet and went to stand by the window. "I hope we don't have another blizzard like that for a long, long time. There were so many things to worry about."

She threw the last bit of her roll to Mikki, who caught it in midair. "But you know that verse in Joshua that we keep coming back to? The Lord used it to remind me that He was taking care of you. Then I prayed that He'd bring it to your mind too."

"Oh? So that's what happened. He did! And I took another look at the whole first chapter of Joshua. After I read about Joshua getting his army ready for battle, I started thinking about our work here. Our warfare. I guess Satan would like to discourage us, but God has given us weapons, like His Word, and the Cessna . . ."

"And some good soldiers," said Liz.

"Right! Tignak. And Samson. And Peter and all the people who are praying for us."

Liz was looking outside, toward Tignak's cabin. "Sarah and the grandmother," she said.

"Yes. And I'm sure He's going to give us some more."

She smiled. "Like maybe the young man out there who's walking down the lane?"

"Who's that?"

"Henry. Oh, good! He's turning onto our path."

Henry had dropped by to welcome Steve back and wanted to ask him about some verses he'd been puzzling over in his Gospel of Mark. Liz made hot tea for them, and they talked for more than an hour.

After he left, Steve turned to Liz. "Now that's exciting! He's reading the Word for himself and really thinking about it. If the Lord gives us a few more like Henry, great things could happen in Koyalik."

That evening, he and Liz and Tignak discussed ideas for helping the young church to grow during the next few months. Tignak would preach on Sunday mornings, and Steve and Liz would take care of the music.

"Tignak," Steve said, "for Christmas, do you think there's any chance we could read the story of Christ's birth in Eskimo?"

"Well, we've only got six weeks, but there's always a chance. We'd have to translate it from the book of Luke." He gave Steve a teasing smile. "If you want to work that hard."

Steve grinned back at him. "Whatever it takes."

"That's a good idea," said Liz. "Let's translate a couple of Christmas carols too. Grandmother is helping me with a new song right now."

They decided that on Sunday evenings Steve and Tignak would have an informal Bible study using the Gospel of

Mark. "Let's keep meeting at my house," said Tignak. "People are getting used to that, I think."

He looked at Liz. "I'm hearing good things about your Story Club. Sounds like the children go home and tell their parents about those Bible stories."

"I'm thankful that Gus lets us have it at the Trading Post after school," said Liz. "The children are already there, and some of them like to hang around for a while."

"He's a good man, that Gus. He really likes the Eskimos; he's different from most white men." Tignak closed his notebook and stood up to leave. "I just wish he were a Christian."

Another storm roared into the village that night, but even with the blowing snow, several families showed up at church the next day. Henry came, and Victor's uncle, and so did Victor, with his three small boys. The boys looked a little more scruffy than usual.

Victor probably wasn't managing very well without Nida, Steve thought. The doctor had said she'd be in the hospital for at least a week, and it would take another couple of weeks before she was really strong again.

When the service ended, Tignak and Sarah took Victor aside to talk to him. Afterwards, Victor came over to shake hands with Steve, smiling broadly. "I worry about my boys," he said. "When I go seal hunting, they all alone. But Tignak say bring them to his house and Sarah take care of them. Very kind!"

In the days that followed, bad weather made it dangerous to fly, and the mail plane came only once, but thanks to Gus's short wave radio, news trickled in from the outside world.

The United States was still trying to negotiate a peace treaty with North Korea. Alaska's governor had made another fiery speech in favor of statehood for Alaska.

Word came from Nome that Nida was improving and had decided to stay there with her sister for a few weeks. Victor's children looked much cleaner these days and seemed to be thriving as part of Tignak's family.

At Shanaluk, Am-nok had died. Charlie went around with a haunted look in his eyes, and Steve grieved for them both.

Meanwhile, Tignak, Victor, and Victor's uncle planned a trip up the coast to hunt for walrus and perhaps get a couple of seals. As soon as the weather cleared, they packed their dogsleds with food, a Primus stove, cans of gasoline for the boat's motor, and their harpoons. On top of it all went their long skin boat, the *umiak*.

The umiak was larger than a kayak, big enough for the three men, but like a kayak, it was made of skin. To Steve it seemed awfully fragile for darting between icebergs, but he reminded himself that these men had hunted this way all their lives.

He and Liz got up early Monday morning to watch the hunters leave. The moon was still high, giving them plenty of light for traveling. A brisk wind blew at their backs, speeding the dog teams northward, and soon they were lost to sight in the glistening expanse of white.

By evening of the next day, they still had not returned. Steve wanted to ask Sarah or Charlie whether this was to be expected, but instead of worrying them, he decided to walk over to the Trading Post and ask Gus.

Gus was stacking cans of peaches on a shelf. "Maybe they went a long ways up the coast. But you never know what's going to happen out there on the ice." He frowned. "Let's give them another day—they took plenty of supplies."

Steve went home to pray with Liz and try to keep busy.

By noon on Wednesday, Gus began organizing dog teams to search for the hunters. "Steve," he said, "if you have time to help us, that plane of yours could be very useful."

Of course he had time. He told Gus that he would radio back to the Trading Post if he sighted the hunters, then he hurried to preheat the Cessna.

Charlie ran up to him. "Want me get battery and oil?"

"Yes, please. Liz has the oil warming on the stove."

It was a relief to do something after the hours of waiting and wondering and praying.

Liz came back with Charlie, carrying the battery and a paper bag. She opened it so he could see the paper, long red ribbons, and bottles inside. "Last night you said you might need these."

"Yes—to drop a message. I hope we get a chance to use them."

Charlie knew what to do with the battery and soon had its cables secured.

"Want to come with me?" Steve asked him.

"Sure!" Charlie smiled for the first time in days.

Steve finished his preflight inspection and said goodbye to Liz. They took off, skis clattering over the frozen snow, and he turned the Cessna north, thankful that the weather was clear for once.

He began by flying up the coast to check the shelf ice. The ragged white shoreline showed no signs of life except for dogsled trails.

He dropped lower and flew in widening circles out over the pack ice. From what Jackson had told him, the Eskimos often hunted out there, past the shelf ice, but it was dangerous because the pack ice was a continually shifting mass. Temperature changes or strong winds could cause the ice to buckle into jumbled ridges fifty or sixty feet high, and the ice itself was never predictably solid. The floes could separate and break apart in minutes, leaving jagged black channels of supercooled seawater.

"Try not to land on the pack ice," Jackson had warned. "An open channel can trap you before you know it, and the surface is so rough you can easily lose a ski. Whatever you do, don't turn your engine off. It's so cold out there, you may never get it started again."

At first Charlie was talkative, but after a while he sat with his face pressed against the window and said nothing. One hand clutched the small ivory fox on his parka. Was he afraid of flying? No, he must be worrying about his father.

Steve touched Charlie's shoulder. The boy jumped, turning wide dark eyes toward him.

"Hey, Charlie," he said over the noise of the engine, "you know what?"

The boy licked his lips. "What?"

"The Lord knows where they are. I've been reminding myself of that. And your father belongs to God. He'll take care of him."

"Then He don't let him . . . die?"

"I don't know what's going to happen," said Steve, "but the Lord tells us to pray when we're in trouble, and I've been praying that He will help us to find them."

Charlie turned back to the window, and Steve banked the plane to fly a crisscross pattern over the area he'd been circling.

He saw a team of dogs without a driver and wondered whose they were. Ten minutes later, as they swung closer to the shelf ice, he caught sight of three black dots.

"Look there, Charlie!"

He took the plane down lower, heading toward the small group. Three men were huddled together. One of them looked up and began to wave.

Charlie lurched forward in his seat. "My fadder!"

"Hang on, boy, we'll go see how they're doing."

Steve circled, looking for a smooth length of ice, then flew low to make another careful check. Cautiously he set the plane down, but it was a bone-jarring landing, and the plane bumped across the ice for a long way before it finally stopped.

Charlie burst out of the plane and ran to join his father. Steve stayed behind to keep the engine running.

The men stumbled toward him. Charlie was asking questions and Tignak was answering, but Steve couldn't hear much over the noise of the engine. While he waited, he took out a piece of the paper Liz had sent and made a rough sketch of where they were.

When the men reached him, Steve checked to make sure that none of them was in urgent need of help; then he said, "I'll radio the Trading Post and tell them where you are. I think we saw your dogs farther south, and there's a rescue team around here somewhere. Stay put and we'll make sure they find you."

Charlie jumped back into the airplane, and Steve made a quick takeoff. Once he was aloft, he radioed the Trading Post, then he swung south to look for one of the rescue teams.

"They glad you come," said Charlie. "They shoot three seals and start back, then Victor see walrus and shoot. But it get mad and rip up boat. They get on ice fast, only a little bit wet. Then ice break off and wind blow them out to sea."

Steve shook his head. "How did they stay alive?"

"They eat seal meat. They make ice block house. Next day they walk and walk. Very cold. Wind blow ice back to land, but they don't know where they are. Dogs gone away somewhere."

Charlie peered out of the window; then he grinned. "Lookit!" He had spotted a rescue team.

"Okay," Steve said. "Put this map into one of those bottles and tie a ribbon on it."

Charlie understood right away. "Can I drop it?"

"Sure. Just don't hit anybody."

He flew low, and Charlie opened the window. Freezing air rushed into the cabin, and Charlie hurriedly dropped the bottle down to the rescue team.

Steve pulled the plane back up to altitude, and together they watched as one of the team picked up the bottle. He checked his fuel gauge. "We'll make a couple more circles to look for those dogs, but then we'd better head for Koyalik. We can always come back out after we get some more gas."

Charlie nodded and glued himself to the window once more.

Steve flew a dozen circles and was just turning back when the engine coughed. It coughed again and began running rough, the hoarse, grating sound that makes a pilot's breath catch in his throat.

Charlie gave him a worried glance. "Something go bad?"

# 9 God's Time

Steve was listening to the engine. "Maybe."

The plane began to lose altitude, and he pushed in the mixture control knob to give the engine as much fuel as possible. That made no change. He checked the two magnetos. When he selected the left magneto, the engine shut off. When he used both, it ran rough again. When he selected only the right magneto, the engine smoothed out.

"Hmm. Something wrong with that left magneto."

For now, the engine could run on just one magneto, but that was a pretty risky way to fly. He glanced at the shoreline to get his bearings. Nome was closer to them than Koyalik, and in Nome there was a mechanic who could look at that magneto.

*Whithersoever.*

He banked the plane and headed back north.

"Where we going?" asked Charlie.

"You ever been to Nome?"

"No!"

"Well, I think we'd better take this Zebra up there and get it fixed. Want to see if you can get Gus on the radio for me?"

"Okay! Like this?" Charlie picked up the microphone, and from the way he handled it, Steve knew the boy had been watching closely every time he used the radio.

"That's it."

When Charlie had reached Gus, he handed over the mike so Steve could explain what they were doing. "And tell Liz not to wait supper. This should take only a couple of hours to fix, but we're almost out of daylight. Hope to see you tomorrow."

They landed at Nome in the fading glow of sunset, and the small white lights on the runway were a welcome sight.

A mechanic promised to have the magneto fixed by morning, and Steve took Charlie to the hotel he'd stayed in the last time. Then, in the dusky half-light of a long Arctic evening, they set out to look around Nome. Steve hunched deep into his parka, glad for its warmth as his face stiffened in the cold.

The main street was only hard-packed snow, but it was lined with brightly lit stores. Charlie strolled through the general store, lingering in fascination at each shelf. He peered into the restaurants and stamped his feet appreciatively on the wooden sidewalks.

Finally they chose a place to eat, and Steve ordered reindeer steaks for both of them. Charlie could hardly eat, he was so busy staring around the restaurant and sizing up the other customers. Many of them were Eskimos or Indians, but a few looked like old-time prospectors, complete with grimy work clothes and ragged beards.

Charlie's eyes sparkled as he listened to a pair of old-timers boast about the gold nuggets they'd mined. Steve watched him, and the small ivory fox that hung from the boy's parka caught his attention. He remembered learning last year how much Charlie depended on his amulets—like that carved fox—to give him good hunting and keep him from being afraid. Perhaps tonight they could have a serious talk.

They lingered over their apple pie, reluctant to leave the restaurant with its bustling warmth and friendly chatter, but finally Charlie began to yawn, and they hurried back through the cold to their hotel room.

After enjoying the luxury of a hot shower, Steve settled down in bed to read his Bible. Charlie, who had exclaimed over the old-fashioned bathroom at the end of the hall and examined each piece of furniture in their room, stretched out on the other bed. He stared at the faded red roses on the wallpaper, and Steve thought he must be almost asleep.

Charlie rolled over onto his stomach. "Why you read that book so much?"

"Because God wrote it," said Steve. "I want to know God."

Charlie sat up, cross-legged on the bed. "Today in the airplane, you not scared."

It was not a question, so Steve waited.

"Before Am-nok die, I talk to him," Charlie said. "I look at his eyes. In old days, he have lotsa power, but at the end he scared."

Absent-mindedly, Charlie picked up the pillow and squeezed it with both hands. In a low voice he asked, "Why Am-nok scared?"

Steve leaned toward him. "The Bible says that all men have done wrong things—they have sinned. And God is holy. I think that's why men are afraid to die. They'll have to answer to a holy God."

"But you always talk about *God loves*."

"Yes, God loves us very much. That's why He sent Jesus Christ, His own Son, to take the punishment for our sins."

Charlie jumped off the bed and pulled the blankets to the floor. "This bed too soft."

He sat on the floor, holding the pillow against his chest. "Lotsa times, men die on the ice. Today when we look down at ice, I feel like cold hands on my back." He sent Steve a shy glance, and his arms tightened around the pillow. "Sometimes I have bad scared feeling inside. It twist and turn like fish caught in net. I hate to be scared. Do you think my fadder scared today?"

Steve smiled. "The other men were probably scared, but I don't think your father was. Why don't you ask him when we get back?"

Charlie nodded; then he became very busy arranging the blankets on the floor. He curled up on top of them, still holding onto the pillow, and seemed to fall asleep instantly.

Steve returned to his reading, but he couldn't keep his mind on it. Charlie frowned as he slept, his body drawn into a tight knot, and Steve wondered what he was dreaming about. "Lord," he prayed, "draw Charlie to Yourself. Set him free from his fear." He thought about the men who had been stranded on the ice and prayed for them too. Perhaps the experience of being so close to death would make Victor or his uncle think more seriously about God.

Finally he switched off the light and went to sleep.

The next morning, heads bent against the icy wind, they hurried down to the North Pole Bakery for breakfast. Steve had hoped Charlie might want to continue last night's conversation, but there was no opportunity. They shared a long table with two sociable pilots and an old miner who was full of tales about the old days.

Charlie asked the men question after question, and as Steve listened to them talk, he prayed silently, "Lord, Your timing is perfect. Let me not be impatient with what You are doing for Charlie."

They flew back to Koyalik under threatening gray skies, and snow was powdering the windshield as they landed. After shutting down the engine, Steve prayed, as he usually did, thanking God for His protection during the trip. This time he prayed aloud for Charlie's benefit.

Liz and Tignak were there to meet them, and they learned that the dogs had been found and the hunters were well, although Victor's uncle limped on swollen feet. Tignak invited Steve and Liz over for a meal that evening, saying that Sarah had cooked it for a celebration.

Victor and his uncle came too, along with Henry and Emma. Victor's three boys, who were still staying at Tignak's house, made a lively addition to the party. Sarah had gone to the trouble of making Eskimo ice cream, a concoction of pounded berries whipped with snow and seal oil. To Steve, it tasted more like seal oil than anything else, but Victor's oldest boy and Charlie ate two bowls apiece.

While they were finishing the ice cream, Liz said, "You know what I don't want to miss this year?"

"What?" said Steve and Charlie together.

"Thanksgiving. Sarah and I have been talking, and this year we want to have a feast. And invite the whole church."

"Well," said Steve with a smile, "here we are."

Everyone laughed, and Liz did too. "Okay, how about everyone in Koyalik who wants to come? We can talk about how the first Thanksgiving started." She waved her spoon in the air. "After all, Alaska is part of the United States, and it might become a state someday. These are American citizens. They should celebrate Thanksgiving."

Victor's uncle smiled, and the laughlines crinkled around his eyes. "Maybe Gus let us use the schoolroom. It is for America. For our country. What is the English word?"

"Patriotic," said Liz. She smiled at him. "Okay. I'll ask Gus, and Sarah and I will make plans. I just wish Nida were here too."

"Maybe in few weeks," said Victor. But it seemed to Steve that he didn't look very hopeful. Was he having trouble convincing Nida that he'd stopped drinking? Had he really stopped?

A few times Steve had thought he smelled beer on Victor's breath, but he wasn't sure. Besides, where would he get the stuff? Gus didn't sell liquor, and the village council had voted to keep liquor out of Koyalik. Even drinking it at home would be breaking the village laws.

Saturday morning, Liz went off to shop at the Trading Post, and Steve decided to study for the test Tignak had promised them. He set out his notebook and dictionary and glanced out the window at the purple twilight of mid-morning. Victor's uncle was limping up the path to their cabin.

Steve asked the man in and served him the customary hot black tea. Liz had left a plate of peanut brittle on the table, and Victor's uncle ate one piece after another, as if he were eating a meal. They talked for a long time, Eskimo fashion, about the weather, seal hunting, and the walrus attack on the hunters' umiak.

Finally Victor's uncle got around to the reason for his visit. "I come to church and hear you talk God's words. I read God's words in Eskimo. Out on the ice I think about God." He paused, his face more solemn than usual, and Steve prayed silently that he would not stop.

At last, the old Eskimo said in a low voice, "I want to belong to God, but I know I have done many sins. There is verse in Mark chapter ten. It say Christ gave His life 'a ransom for many.' Did He make payment for my sins?"

Steve put his hand on the man's arm and tried to think of the right Eskimo words. "Yes, He did," he said in Eskimo. "God loves you very much, and it makes His heart happy that you are coming to Him."

He glanced at his desk, at the prayer in Eskimo that Tignak had helped him to compose. "Let me show you some more verses in God's Word. After that, we will pray, and you can talk to Christ yourself."

They prayed together, and then Steve took a red Bible from the stack on his shelf.

"This book is for you," he said. "It is written in English, but I think you will find it helpful as you study."

Victor's uncle beamed as he turned its pages. *"Kuyana!* (Thank you!)" he exclaimed. "Now I have all of God's Word for my own."

After Victor's uncle left, Steve sat down at his desk and bowed his head over the scattered papers. "Thank You, Father. Thank You for delivering this man from darkness! Bless him richly and draw many more to Yourself."

I've got to tell Liz, he thought. Whistling, he set off to find her.

That afternoon when Tignak came for language study, Steve told him the good news about Victor's uncle.

Tignak smiled. "Wonderful! I'm glad you could speak to him in Eskimo. And you used the Eskimo prayer too! I think it's important for Eskimos to pray in Eskimo so they know that this isn't just the white man's religion."

Tignak looked off into the distance, still smiling, and his weather-beaten face glowed like a piece of polished wood.

I've never seen him like this, Steve thought. He's sitting there just smiling and smiling. He glanced at Liz. She had noticed too.

Tignak must have felt Steve's gaze, for he gave him a sparkling glance. "I wasn't going to say anything for a while, but I have to tell you two what happened."

He put his pen down and leaned back in his chair. "Charlie came to me last night, after he'd slept half the day. You really wore him out on that trip, Steve, and you gave him plenty to think about. He had questions about the Bible, and we talked. This isn't the first time we've talked, but before he was sort of testing me, and now he seemed ready to listen. He asks hard questions."

"I know," said Steve.

"Well, it was getting late and I was tired, but he kept on and on. Finally I suggested that we could talk some more in the morning. 'No,' he said, 'I want to belong to God before I go to sleep.' "

Liz grabbed Steve's arm.

Tignak grinned at them. "That woke me right up, I can tell you. He meant it. We prayed together, and last night he asked Christ to be his Savior."

Steve sat for a moment in silence. God's time. At last!

Tignak was still talking. "But we need to keep praying for him, and this is why I'm not running around shouting—Charlie is still wearing that fox amulet of his."

"Doesn't he have some owl claws too?" asked Liz.

"He used to, but they seem to have disappeared. The fox amulet, though, is really important to him. Am-nok carved it. He hangs onto it because he thinks it will make him brave."

Tignak ran a hand through his thinning black hair. "Those things look harmless, but they're not. He's depending on that animal's spirit to give him courage."

Steve nodded, understanding. "Until he gets rid of it, he won't grow as a Christian. He's still under Satan's influence, in a way. I'd hate for him to think he can be like the people at Mierow Lake, trying to mix Christianity with the old Eskimo beliefs."

"Exactly." Tignak looked grave.

Steve smiled at him. "But look what God has done! We'll keep on praying."

# 10 A Tool in God's Hand

On Monday the mail plane came early and left almost immediately. Mack was the pilot. Steve could tell by the way he handled the plane. And if Mack was in a hurry to leave, he was probably trying to outrun a storm.

Sure enough, the forecast was for more bad weather. By the time Steve returned from picking up their mail, snow was whirling across the village, driven by a biting wind.

He pulled the cabin door shut behind him with relief and kicked a rug up against it to keep out the draft. "Looks like some more letter writing and language study weather," he said.

Liz looked up from the table where she was working. "Any mail?"

"Two from Chicago and one from Peter. The doctor is pleased with that operation they did on his leg. He told Peter that if he keeps on improving, he'll be able to fly again someday."

"Someday? Well, that's better than never." Liz smiled. "You know what? I have a feeling that the Lord knows we need Peter back here *soon*, not someday. And He's going to surprise that doctor."

"It can't happen too soon for me," said Steve.

He stepped over to the table to see what she was doing. She was using colored pencils and paint on a large sheet of paper.

# *Have not I commanded*

"Hey," he said. "That's our verse."

"Yes. I'm going to glue it onto some cardboard and hang it up where we can see it. We could use it at the Thanksgiving feast too, sort of like a motto."

"Pretty long for a motto."

"Okay!" She poked him in the stomach. "Our verse, then. And do you think you could get us a caribou? It's going to take a lot of meat to feed all these people."

"As soon as this storm blows away," said Steve. "Maybe I can go hunting with one of the men."

Liz's plans for the Thanksgiving celebration worked out just as they'd hoped. Gus let them use the schoolroom at the Trading Post, and Steve and Charlie each shot a caribou, so there was plenty to eat. Liz hung her poster at the front of the room. The brightly colored verse drew everyone to read it and ask questions. More people came to eat and visit and trade stories than had ever come to church, and they stayed for half the night.

The Sunday after Thanksgiving, Henry showed up at church with three cousins. After his relatives left, he and Tignak sat and talked by the stove for a long time.

Steve went into the kitchen, where Liz and the grandmother were fixing the Sunday meal, and the three of them prayed for Henry.

Steve was stirring a pot of soup when Tignak came into the kitchen with Henry.

"Steve, this young man has something to tell you," Tignak said in Eskimo.

Henry leaped forward and grabbed Steve's hand. "Now I belong to Christ! I want to know all about God."

Steve took Henry's hand in both of his and shook it. "That's great news! I hope you will come see me this afternoon, and we can talk."

The young Eskimo's brown eyes glowed.

"God is so good!" Steve said in Eskimo.

Henry looked surprised, and immediately Steve wondered whether he'd said what he meant to.

Henry turned to Tignak and asked a rapid-fire question in Eskimo.

"Oh, no!" said Steve, sure now that he had blundered.

Tignak answered Henry, gestured at Steve with a smile, and took Henry out of the room, still talking.

When Tignak returned, Steve gave him a rueful smile. "Guess I'd better stick to English for a while longer."

"No harm done," said Tignak. "I know what you meant to say, but it came out sounding like 'God is nothing.' I explained, and I'm sure Henry understands."

He grinned at Steve. "I think we'd better do a lot more talking together in Eskimo. You know what to say, but sometimes it does sound a bit peculiar."

When Henry came to visit that afternoon, Steve presented him with one of the red Bibles from the bookshelf and showed him where the Book of Mark was. Then both

Henry and Tignak worked with Steve and Liz, practicing the complicated art of conversing in Eskimo.

"Well, you're improving," Tignak finally said. "I think I'll leave you in Henry's capable hands for the rest of this week. I really want to make another trip to Shanaluk."

"Want me to take you over in the Cessna?"

"No, I just want to talk quietly with Joseph and a few others, and they might not be as receptive if I come flying in there like a white man."

Tignak returned four days later, exhausted from the bitter cold and uneasy about his old friends. "The people seem to be drifting in all directions. At least when Am-nok was alive they had a leader, and not a bad one at that. But now . . . what's that expression? They're like sheep without a shepherd. Some are clinging to the old traditions. A few of the young people have already moved to Nome, to the big city where they can make lots of money."

He sighed. "I'm ready to preach, and they don't want to listen." He looked at Steve. "You still thinking about another trip to Mierow Lake?"

"I sure am. I really want to get back there as soon as I can. At least one of the men is a believer, and a few others seem to be on the right track. They have lots of questions, like Charlie."

"Okay, let's make some plans."

Liz thought she should keep up with her Story Club, so Tignak and Steve decided to go alone.

Charlie wanted to come too. Steve shook his head. "I wish you could, but the plane has a lot to carry with all our gear and full gas tanks. It won't fly if it's too heavy."

Charlie nodded, but Steve could tell he was disappointed. "Next time, if your father agrees, okay?"

When he'd finished packing for the trip, Steve walked over to his bookshelf. Peter had sent them five red Bibles. One had gone to Tignak. Another had gone to Victor's uncle, and just last week he'd given one to Henry. Samson would get the fourth Bible. He took down Samson's Bible and eyed the one that was left. For Jackson, in God's time.

They took off on a cloudy Monday morning as soon as there was enough light to see to the end of the airstrip. They had only four hours of murky light in the short December day, but Steve thought that should be plenty of time.

*I hope nothing slows us down,* Steve thought. *It's going to be great to see Samson again and give him that Bible.*

They soon left Koyalik behind, and he filed a flight plan as usual, then checked on the weather. Skies would be clearing along his route, they predicted.

"Well, that's good," Steve said to Tignak. "But in the mountains you never know what kind of weather you'll run into."

Sure enough, during the next hour, dark clouds began to pile up on the horizon. As Old Man's Hat came into sight, the wind grew stronger, and the little plane began to bounce.

The clouds grew so thick that soon they were flying through gray mist. Steve checked his heading and climbed higher, trying to find a way out.

He glanced at Tignak. "Got your seat belt on tight?"

"Yes." Tignak looked calm as ever. Maybe, compared to hunting walrus in a skin boat, this didn't seem very bad.

Snow began to fall, driven by a strong headwind, and the windshield frosted over. Steve kept an eye on the airspeed indicator. The plane was definitely flying more slowly. He pushed in the throttle, hoping to keep the airspeed up, and peered through the side window. A rough white film of ice had formed on the strut.

"Decision time, Tignak. We're getting ice, and pretty soon we'll be too heavy to fly. Should we find a place to land or try to run for home?"

"Your choice. I've been praying."

"I don't really want to play Boy Scout tonight," Steve said. "Let's head back to Koyalik." He eased the plane into a wide, shallow turn. With this weight of ice, it would stall if he turned too fast. The wind was behind them now; maybe they could fly out of this stuff.

He squinted at the snow through the small part of the windshield that wasn't frosted over. The plane rocked from side to side, shuddering in the wind, but every minute should be taking them farther away from the storm.

He reached for the microphone. "Galena radio, Cessna 1577 Zebra."

"77 Zebra—Galena—go ahead."

"Roger, we've run into some pretty bad weather. Please cancel my flight plan to Mierow Lake. I'm heading back toward Koyalik. If I don't make it, I'll try to land somewhere along the way."

"Roger, 77 Zebra. Good luck, Steve."

The plane bucked violently, and he dropped the mike to work with the controls. He caught a glimpse of tundra. At least they were out of the mountains.

The dark shapes of caribou slipped past below them.

If he could see caribou, the snow must be thinning, but he was much too low.

He pushed in the throttle, and he pulled up the nose with care. The Cessna climbed sluggishly, heavy with ice. Just a little farther.

He tried to plan ahead. It was a dark day, still blowing snow, and he was going to have trouble finding the airstrip at Koyalik.

He called Gus on the radio and handed the mike to Tignak. "Tell him what's happening. Ask him to get some men out on the airstrip with lanterns. We should be there in ten minutes."

He tipped the nose of the Cessna down, just a little, to maintain his airspeed. With all the ice he was carrying, he wanted to descend gradually, but if he slowed the plane too much, it would fall out of the sky,

"See Koyalik anywhere?"

"Yes, over on your left," said Tignak.

Steve gave the village a fleeting glance. A pair of tiny lights twinkled up at him through the gloom. "Good for you, Gus," he muttered. "Okay. We're going in."

The Cessna sank lower and lower toward the ground, dropped heavily onto the runway, and seemed to slide forever before it stopped. Steve shut down the engine, and they sat in a silence that was broken only by the soft patter of snow on the windshield and the metallic clicks of the cooling engine.

He rested his forehead against the control wheel. No Mierow Lake this time. Samson wouldn't get his Bible. And those kindly people would keep on with their rules, missing the truth.

"Too bad," said Tignak, as if he knew what Steve was thinking.

"Yes, I'm disappointed," said Steve. The Book of Joshua came to mind. "But the Lord's been showing me that our work here is a battle against the power of evil, a spiritual warfare. I have to keep reminding myself that He's the one directing the campaign. He gave us this airplane, so if He decides not to use it, that's okay." Steve lifted his head to gaze at the snow-powdered windshield. "And it's no small thing that He brought us back safely."

Tignak turned to look at him. "I like that thought: God as our Commander. I'm sure Satan has engineered a lot of opposition here to His work." The old Eskimo smiled. "But nothing will stop our God: not bad weather, not a powerful shaman, not any schemes of evil men."

They prayed together then, thanking God for a safe return and asking Him for strength and wisdom in the next battle. Cold crept into the cockpit and turned their words to frozen vapor, but Steve's disappointment eased.

He and Tignak pulled the plane off the airstrip and tied it down.

"Do you hear that?" Tignak stopped and looked up into the darkness.

All Steve could hear was the rushing wind.

Tignak cocked his head. "There—again."

Above the wind came the buzzing of a plane's engine.

"Sounds like Jackson's Cub." Steve glimpsed the small yellow plane high above them. "He's circling! Let's get those lanterns back over here."

But Jackson had already lined up with the runway and was coming in fast.

# 11 That Weasel

The yellow Cub plowed down the runway, its skis following the faint tracks left by Steve's plane. It came to a stop at the far end, and Steve ran down to make sure everything was okay.

Jackson climbed out of the cockpit, shaking his head. "Sure am glad to be here in one piece! Nice of someone to land just before me. Was that you, Steve?"

"Yup. I just got down by the skin of my teeth. How come you're here?"

"I was on my way home, but the weather closed in, and I picked up a bunch of ice. Decided to pay you a visit."

"Come on over as soon as you get a chance," said Steve.

"Thanks. I sure will."

Jackson would be staying in the room at the Trading Post that Gus kept for pilots, so Steve and Tignak unloaded the Cessna and went home to their families.

Liz met him at the cabin door. "I've been praying for you all day. When that storm hit, I hoped you weren't trying to fly through it. Then I heard you go over."

"The Lord is merciful! Those men and their lanterns were a big help," said Steve. "Jackson got caught in it too. He came in behind me."

"I thought I heard his Cub." She hurried to make supper, and Steve sank into a chair. He flexed his fingers, wiggling the stiffness out of them. *I must have been hanging onto that control wheel with a death grip,* he thought.

After supper he unpacked his duffle bag and put Samson's Bible back on the shelf with regret. "Lord, protect Samson," he prayed, "and keep him reading that Gospel of Mark. Please take us back there soon."

That evening Jackson came over for coffee, but he couldn't seem to sit still. He paced the small cabin, mug in hand, pausing from time to time to look out the window. "Snow on top of snow on top of snow," he muttered. "Why did I ever leave Texas?"

He stopped to read the verse on Liz's poster, then paused beside the bookshelf and studied the titles. "You've got two of those red Bibles left," he said. "I guess Tignak got one. What happened to the others?"

Steve came to stand beside him. "Victor's uncle accepted Christ about a month ago, so I gave him one. And just last week, Henry became a believer. They'll both study the English version along with the Gospels of Mark you brought us."

He picked up the Bible on top. "This one is for Samson—you know, the guy in Mierow Lake who had all the questions?"

"Yeah, I remember Samson. That's good, Steve, really good." Jackson's voice was unusually serious.

Then he grinned. "So who's the lucky guy that gets the last one?"

"I've been hanging onto that one." Steve kept his voice light. "It's got your name on it. Just thought you might want to take a look at it sometime."

Jackson turned back to the table without comment. He rubbed at the scar on his face. "You got any more of that peanut brittle, Liz? Reminds me of when I was a kid."

He dropped into a chair, and Liz refilled his mug with coffee. Jackson stayed late that night, more talkative than Steve had ever seen him. He told them a war story Steve hadn't heard before, about an island in the South Pacific that had a large ranch on it. Because of the war, the cattle had been set free to roam the island, and sometimes they were shot down during Japanese air raids.

"So a retired Navy man set up a restaurant he called South Pacific Joe's Hamburger Spot," said Jackson. "He turned those butchered cattle into hamburger, and every time the Japanese went over, he had a fresh supply of meat." Jackson grinned, remembering. "Joe could whip up a pretty good powdered-milk shake, too. We used to make excuses to land on that island so we could eat at Joe's."

Without pausing for breath, Jackson switched from the South Pacific to Alaska and began describing the narrow escapes of bush pilots he knew. Perhaps he'd been more worried about today's landing than he would admit.

Finally he got to his feet. "Well, I've finished up all the peanut brittle and half the cookies, so I guess I'd better get going."

He pulled on his flight jacket and smiled at Liz as he slipped a bag of cookies into the pocket. "Thanks for the extras. They'll sure taste good tomorrow."

He glanced at Steve. "Might as well take that Bible off your hands too, while I'm at it."

Steve handed him the book.

"Thanks." Jackson gave him a swift glance and banged out into the night.

As soon as he'd gone, Liz exclaimed, "Hey, do you think he'll read it?"

"I don't think he'd pretend," Steve said. "I think he's more interested than he'd admit right now. It's not only the Eskimos who struggle with fear."

He whistled a tuneless little song as he went outside for an armful of wood. When he returned Liz said, "Oh, you know what? I was so excited about your getting back that I forgot to tell you something."

He put a few more sticks of wood into the stove, and she curled up on the bed. "Sarah and I went fishing for tomcod this morning," she said. "I caught more than sixty!"

"Well, Mikki will love you for that!" Tomcod was a small fish, easily snared and used mostly for dog food, but Liz liked to think that they were great sport.

"You know how all the old ladies sit on their sleds next to the holes in the ice? Well, Sarah and I had been fishing for a while and I was listening to what everybody was saying—and understanding only half of it, of course—"

Steve sat down beside her. Liz always seemed to get useful information from her friends.

"And a couple of them started talking about their husbands and how worried they were, because the husbands were *something*. I didn't know what that expression meant.

"I whispered to Sarah and she said, 'Wasting money.'

" 'What are they wasting money on?' I asked. She listened for a while and asked a few questions, then shook her head at me to be quiet."

Steve grinned. "She expected you to be quiet?"

"But I was!" Liz said. "I didn't say a word until we were back here taking care of the fish. Then she told me that a couple of the men have been buying beer from Mack, on the sly."

Steve's grin faded. "And Victor is probably one of them." He jumped to his feet and paced back and forth. "I thought the village council voted to keep Koyalik dry."

"They did. That's one of the things I like about this village."

"I think I'd better talk to Gus."

The next afternoon, even though the storm hadn't let up, Steve plowed through waist-high drifts to the Trading Post. He found Jackson and Gus trading war stories.

"Well, come on in, stranger," said Gus. "Pour yourself some coffee and sit down." He started off on his favorite bush pilot yarn, which Steve had already heard twice.

When he finished, Jackson said, "That reminds me. I don't get over here much now that they've got me flying charter. How's Mack working out?"

"Well, he's not good for much, in my opinion," said Gus. "But he does get the freight in and out." The old trader chuckled. "You know how the kids used to help you? He hates them, says they're all thieving little rats, so he has to carry everything up here by himself."

"I hear he's doing a little bootlegging these days," Steve said quietly.

Gus's forehead turned red. "I wondered about that! All of a sudden he seems much too friendly with a couple of the men."

"Is Victor in that bunch?" Something ached, deep inside Steve.

"Yah." Gus frowned. "Well, maybe no, not lately, I guess. Vic's kind of been keeping to himself the last week or two."

Gus stood up to refill his mug with coffee and banged the pot back down onto the stove. "The next time that weasel shows his face in here, I am going to tell him a thing or two."

"The company doesn't like pilots using their planes for things like that," muttered Jackson.

Steve stayed for a while longer, then bought some groceries, and headed outside. He bent low to keep his face out of the wind, and his feet dragged through the fresh snow. Not Victor! At their cabin door, he paused to stomp the snow off his mukluks. What could he do to help him?

Liz started putting away the food he'd bought. "So what did Gus say?"

"He hit the roof. He's going to talk to Mack."

"You know what?" Liz stopped, a can of green beans in her hand. "Mack's an evil man. It makes sense that Satan would use him to fight us."

"You're right. Satan would love to discourage our little church." Steve put a kettle of water on the stove. "I'm going to get Tignak and a couple of the men together. Maybe we can meet tomorrow night. We need to pray for Victor and the whole situation."

Thursday, the storm lifted. Jackson flew off, and Mack flew in with the mail. Steve saw Gus tramping down to the airstrip to meet Mack, but he didn't hang around to watch.

Sunday's service went well, and afterwards Steve's small group of men decided to meet every other night for prayer. Steve and Tignak made plans to fly over to Shanaluk on Monday afternoon for a brief visit. "Tignak's really worried about Shanaluk," Steve told Liz. "I'm praying that something good will happen today."

Monday morning, he and Tignak brushed the snow off the Cessna, and while Steve was pre-warming the engine, the mail plane landed.

Mack unloaded the freight without a glance in their direction and started off for the Trading Post. With his high-topped leather boots and long legs, he moved quickly through the deep snow and soon returned.

"Our friend must be in a hurry," said Tignak, watching the takeoff. "I wonder why."

The flight to Shanaluk went faster than usual because of a brisk tailwind. Steve made two passes over the frozen lake before finding a stretch of ice that looked smooth enough to land on, but even then, the skis rattled and bumped over the rough, rippled ice. They tied down the plane with particular care because of the wind.

"Let's walk toward Joseph's house and see who's around," said Steve.

They pushed through the icy snowdrifts that edged the lake and soon reached a wide, snow-packed trail that wound past the cabins.

One or two of Tignak's old friends spoke in greeting, but most people ignored the two visitors. A man passed them, walking with an odd, lurching gait, and stumbled into a cabin. He was carrying a long-necked brown bottle.

Tignak had noticed it too. He slanted a glance at Steve and shook his head.

Two teenagers paused to talk with Tignak. They asked about the airplane, and Tignak started telling them why Steve had come to Shanaluk.

An older man, heavily muffled in furs, stopped to listen, and Steve began hoping that Tignak might get a chance to preach.

A pair of men sauntered past, then they came back and stood at the edge of the group. They made loud comments and Steve didn't catch all their words, but he understood "go home" and "white man." Finally the men moved off, but the teenagers beside Tignak stared after them, and the older man muttered angrily.

For a while longer, Tignak spoke with them in rapid Eskimo. A gust of wind made Steve glance at the clouds scudding overhead, and, thinking about the weather, he gave up trying to follow the conversation.

A young boy came running down the path from the direction of the lake. "*Ting-ng un!*" he cried. "*Ting-ng un!*"

Steve knew that word. *Airplane.* He ran through the snow to the lake. The Cessna was no longer tied down; it was sliding sideways across the ice.

# 12 Bad Cannon

Steve shouted in exasperation and scrambled out across the frozen lake. A gust of wind tipped the Cessna up on one side and a wing tip grazed the ice. The tie-down ropes trailed behind it.

By the time he caught up with the plane, it had buried its nose in a snowdrift at the other end of the lake. He grabbed one of the icy tie-down ropes and pulled, but he could not move it out of the drift.

Tignak arrived while Steve was still staring at the plane. "Thought I did a better job of tying her up," he muttered.

Tignak glanced at the rope. "That's been cut."

Steve looked down at the rope in his hand. "You're right." He coiled up the rope and threw it into the plane. "So . . . the battle goes on."

Several men had gathered around, and they helped pull the plane out of the snow. Steve examined the propeller first, then walked slowly around the plane, checking for damage. The landing gear and underbelly seemed to be okay.

*Thank you, Lord, for watching over us.*

He looked up at the clouds. "I was thinking we'd better leave before the weather closes down, anyway."

Tignak agreed, and they climbed into the Cessna. As they flew, Tignak remained silent for such a long time that Steve glanced over to see what was the matter.

The old Eskimo was staring out of the window, his face grim. Finally he spoke. "I found out a few things today. There is liquor available in Shanaluk, and quite a few men are buying it." His voice grew rough with anger. "Do you know what liquor does to an Eskimo? He forgets all his heritage of social responsibility and self-control. He goes out of his mind."

"Gus told me," said Steve. "It'll tear Shanaluk apart." He thought about Victor and felt the weight of oppression that he'd sensed in Am-nok's cabin.

Koyalik came into sight, and he silently lined up his approach, still thinking about what Tignak had said. After they landed, he asked, "Did they tell you where they're getting the stuff?"

"They said a pilot brings it into Shanaluk when he delivers the mail. He sells it at a pretty steep price. Guess who."

"Our new pilot must be making a tidy profit," Steve said. "I wonder if Mack moved his operation from Koyalik to Shanaluk."

"Could be. But a warning from Gus won't impress him for long. He'll sneak the stuff back into Koyalik if he gets a chance." Tignak sighed. "I think we need to do a lot more praying."

On Thursday, Steve noticed that Mack arrived late in the afternoon and left his plane tied down at the edge of the airstrip. Either he was waiting for a passenger or he had engine trouble. Or he was up to something.

Steve stopped by the Trading Post after supper, but nothing seemed out of the ordinary. Gus said that Mack had walked through earlier, had spoken briefly to the men sitting around the stove, and had gone upstairs to the pilots' room.

Since Victor was at the Trading Post with his boys, Steve talked with them for a while. Victor soon left, saying that Sarah was strict about getting the children to bed early.

Victor looked lonely, Steve thought. It was kind of Tignak to open his home to Victor's children, and Sarah was doing a good job, but those boys needed their mother. Maybe Nida would come back soon.

He returned to his cabin, refilled the wood box, and worked late on his message for Sunday's service. He was turning down the lantern for the night when Liz whispered to him. "Steve? Something outside . . ."

He stepped to the window. Someone was crawling up the path to their cabin. He ran to open the door, and Victor fell across the threshold.

Steve bent to help him stand, and the sour odor of beer filled his nostrils. He put an arm around the man. "Come, sit by the stove. Liz, better make some tea—make it good and strong."

Victor dropped heavily into the chair and groaned. "No-o-o. Not drunk, Steve."

Liz turned up the lantern, and Steve searched Victor's face. It was swollen and bloodied, but his eyes were clear. What was going on here?

Liz brought a bowl of water and a cloth. Gently she wiped the blood from his face. "Victor, why do you smell so awful?"

"Mack throw beer at me. He throw it all over my house." His face twisted in pain. "My arm. I think he break it. My knee—"

"Okay, no more questions until we get you fixed up," said Steve. Cold anger swept through him, clearing his mind and moving him to action. "Liz, can you get us a pair of my pants and a shirt?"

He stripped off the caribou skins that Victor had been wearing, threw them outside, and helped him into clean clothes. Then he checked Victor's injuries: a badly bruised knee, a wrenched and bruised arm, a swollen jaw, and a cut over one eye.

Liz brought tea, and Victor drank two mugs full, scalding hot, before he stopped shivering.

"Thank you," he said. "Now I tell you." He looked at his empty mug, and Liz filled it again. "You know Mack sell beer in Koyalik. For a while I buy it. Then I stop. I know it make me crazy—a bad man."

He lifted his mug and took another long drink. "Some other men still buy it, and some families have trouble. Gus find out and talk to Mack, so Mack stop. Good, I think. Now things get better in Koyalik."

He passed a hand over his swollen jaw. "Tonight Mack see me at Trading Post and he say, 'I come talk to you at your house tonight.' So he come. He tell me I can make lotsa money. Buy phonograph. Buy pretty things for Nida, make her happy."

Victor looked at the floor. "He ask me to help him with beer. He hide it here in old cabin. And he want to start store in Shanaluk. Lotsa people there want to buy beer."

Steve bit back an exclamation. He waited while Victor drained his mug again. "I tell him no," Victor said. "No more beer for me. And I will not help him. He say bad things to me. What is *idiot?*"

"A man who is foolish."

"Oh. I think it mean something worse than that, something really bad. Anyway, he call me idiot, and we fight a little bit. Good thing my kids not there. I hit him hard. He knock me down with chair and kick me. I stay down. He pour beer over me and my house." Victor winced, remembering. "He go away, but not very fast."

Steve leaned back in his chair. "We haven't heard the last of Mack, I'm sure. If he's still got beer stashed at Koyalik, he's pretty serious about the whole business. Where did you say he keeps it?"

"That old place falling down near airstrip."

"Okay. You'd better stay here with us tonight," Steve said. "That man is a loose cannon."

Victor frowned. "Cannon?"

"It's a big gun. And when it's rolling around loose, you don't know what kind of damage it will do."

"Yes, bad cannon."

Before they went to bed, Steve propped a chair under the latch of their door, and for the first time wished that it had a lock.

He got up several times in the night to check on Victor, who was mumbling and groaning in his sleep. *I hope he doesn't have a head injury,* he thought. *That must have been some fight. I wonder what Mack looks like.*

Each time Steve returned to his sleeping bag, he prayed for wisdom to handle the situation tomorrow, and each time the reminder came back: *Thou hast girded me with strength unto the battle.*

At dawn, he awoke to loud banging on their door. It was Mack.

"Liz, you and Victor stay inside." Steve took his time pulling on his boots and zipping up his parka. Mack was making enough noise to waken the whole village, and if anything happened, he wanted to have witnesses.

He went out into the bitter cold and closed the door firmly behind himself.

Mack started shouting in Steve's face, but he looked as if he could hardly stand up, so Steve stepped around him and walked down the path into the wide lane.

Mack limped after him. "Where's that Eskimo friend of yours? You're hiding a thief, Mister Missionary. C'mon, bring him out here so I can talk to him."

Steve shrugged. "A thief?"

Tignak and Charlie had come out of their cabin, pulling on parkas. Steve stopped beside them and quietly told Tignak what had happened.

"Sure he's a thief," yelled Mack. "Stole the lights off my airplane last night. You can go down and look for yourself." He drew a panting breath and winced in pain. "Yeah, he sneaked down there in the middle of the night and pulled them off. I'm taking him to the police in Nome."

"I don't think so," said Steve.

Mack took a step closer, lifted an arm, and almost lost his balance. His face was covered with bruises and cuts. One eye was swollen shut, and the other was turning black. "It was Victor Norlik. I saw him."

"Mack, you've been drinking some of your own beer," said Steve. "Why don't you go back to the Trading Post and sober up?"

By now a crowd of Eskimos had gathered in the lane. Sarah had come outside too and was whispering to Tignak.

Mack cursed loudly.

"Victor spent the night with me," said Steve. "And before that I heard you had a little discussion with him. How come you took beer into his house?"

Mack looked offended. "That's my private business."

Out of the corner of his eye, Steve saw Charlie start off for the Trading Post. He must be going for Gus.

Tignak stepped forward. "It is not your private business that you've carried liquor into Koyalik again." His voice rang through the icy air. "You were warned. Our council has voted to keep the village dry, and you have broken the village law."

All five council members were here, Steve realized: Victor's uncle, Henry, Tignak, and two others. He hardly recognized his jovial neighbors. Each man carried a gun or a long skinning knife, and their dark faces looked threatening.

"And now you're taking liquor into Shanaluk." Tignak's eyes blazed. "You are not welcome in this village. You will find it decidedly uncomfortable if you fly back into Koyalik for any reason."

The councilmen and a dozen others advanced on the pilot, and he backed step by step down the lane.

They had almost reached the airstrip when Mack halted, swaying, and looked over their heads.

"Gus!" he shouted to the tall figure striding toward them. "Gus, c'mon over here." He shot a furious glance at Steve. "This is all your fault. I'm going to report that you're disrupting this village and imposing your religion on these people."

# 13 Was That a Bear?

Gus's long legs carried him swiftly to the edge of the crowd. "What's the problem?" he asked in his deep voice. "Whew! What happened to you, Mack? Tangle with a bear?"

No one moved. No one smiled.

Mack sighed noisily. "Victor Norlik stole my navigation lights, and this fanatic here is protecting him—but I can prove it. I'll bet those lights are in Norlik's cabin, right where he hid them. Let's go and—"

Tignak interrupted. "You know they're in his cabin, right where you hid them."

"You can't prove—"

"We have a witness. Someone saw you go into Victor's cabin with a flashlight at 2:15 this morning. While Victor was staying with Steve."

A murmur ran through the crowd. Several men shifted their guns.

Mack looked from face to face, his blue eyes glittering with dislike. One hand moved to his pocket. Was he carrying a pistol?

"Victor's cabin, eh?" said Gus. "Got to be careful about things like that. People might think you're a bear, stealing something, and shoot you quite by accident."

"Gus, these people are threatening me. Look at them! I'm an American citizen, and I'm going to report—"

"Well, it's their village, Mack. And they're American citizens too." The old trader shrugged. "Looks to me like this bunch of citizens is getting a little unhappy."

"But my nav lights—"

"You don't need them. It's daylight," said Steve.

Gus brushed at the frost forming on his beard. "If I were you, Mack, I'd forget the lights and fly out of here while you're still in one piece. Hey, *was* that a bear you ran into?"

Mack glared at him and limped the rest of the way to his airplane. The crowd followed, watching silently as he prewarmed the engine and did a hurried preflight.

The deep-throated roar of another engine cut through the chill dawn and made Steve look behind him. A tractor was grinding down the lane, gathering speed as it came. The driver was Tignak, and he looked more fierce than Steve had ever seen him.

The tractor rumbled past them and lurched through the snow toward a ramshackle hut that stood beside the airstrip. Tignak didn't stop. He raised the tractor's enormous scoop and plowed straight into the hut. It sagged, leaning slowly to one side.

"Hey!" yelled Mack.

Tignak swung the tractor around and took another run at the hut. This time it toppled sideways. The tractor rolled across the boxes inside, splintering them to ruins.

Mack started forward, but Henry prodded him back to the plane with the tip of his knife. Minutes later, the plane took off and climbed steeply into the sky.

Steve watched it out of sight, but he felt no joy. Mack's cache of liquor had been destroyed, but the man would probably be back on Monday with a new scheme in mind.

A cutting wind soon dispersed the crowd, and Steve walked back up the lane with Gus.

"I don't think Mack's boss wants that kind of pilot flying for him," said Gus in a low voice. "Jackson told me to let him know if the man stepped an inch out of line. He'll be interested in this."

"Come back to my cabin," said Steve. "Maybe we can fill you in on some details. Tignak? Could you and your children come too?"

While Gus sipped coffee, Steve told him how Victor had come to them the night before, and then Victor described what happened between him and Mack.

Steve looked at Tignak. "What's this about a witness?"

Tignak smiled. "Tell him, Sarah."

Sarah spoke from where she sat beside Liz. "Last night I put Victor's boys in bed like every night. Then I go to sleep too. In middle of night, baby cries. A bad dream, I think. So I hold him and we look out the window and I sing to him."

She glanced at Victor. "Victor's cabin is dark, but I see someone go in there."

Gus leaned forward. "Could you tell who the man was?"

"He is not Victor. He is very tall. Wears boots from the States."

Gus nodded, and she went on.

"A little light come on, like flashlight. Then pretty quick, he leave. Where is Victor, I wonder."

Gus glanced at Victor. "You slept here, right?"

"Yes."

"This morning when the man make trouble for Victor, I remember. I tell my fadder."

After they had talked for a while longer, Gus stood up. "Well, the children will think this is a holiday if I don't get over to school pretty soon. Victor, you'd better not go into your cabin until we can go there together. We'll take a witness and see where Mack planted those nav lights."

"Planted?" Victor frowned.

"Yes, he probably put them in a certain place so you'd be blamed for taking them." Gus smiled. "You don't read enough spy stories, Vic. See you later, okay?"

That evening Gus and Victor showed Steve the navigation lights they had found under some caribou skins in Victor's cabin.

"I could plant better." Victor sounded indignant. "First thing, we look there."

Steve picked up the plastic bag of red, green, and white lights. "Why did he ever think you would steal them?"

"They can be sold rather easily," Gus said. "Navigation lights are required on boats as well as on airplanes." He put a hand on the young Eskimo's shoulder. "Speaking of planes, did Victor tell you the good news about Nida?"

Victor smiled. "She come back Monday. She fly in with mail plane." He glanced sideways at Gus. "I hope Mack don't know who she is."

"He doesn't pay much attention to his passengers," said Gus. "I wouldn't worry."

When the mail plane came in on Monday, Mack was not flying it. The new pilot was an older man who didn't have much to say, but he smiled at the children and let them help carry the freight. Nida looked well, Steve thought, and she seemed happy to see her husband and children again.

That evening Liz spoke aloud the question that had been on Steve's mind all day. "I wonder what happened to Mack?"

"Jackson will know," said Steve. "He's coming for Christmas, right?"

"Right. Oh! That's the day after tomorrow, and I still have a hundred things to do!"

Steve grinned. "Sounds normal. At least you've got those new carols ready. And we've finished translating the Christmas story. I can't wait to see their faces when they hear Tignak read it."

"What? No angels and shepherds in costumes?"

"Not this year. It's going to be different enough for them as it is. You'll make a feast, right?"

"Yes, with help from Nida and Emma. I learned how to make mincemeat, so there will be Christmas pies too. We're having a lot of people and their children. And Jackson."

Steve smiled at her enthusiasm. "Remember last year when nobody came?"

"Yes, the Lord has been good to us." Liz bent over a pile of dried willow sticks on the table.

"What's that?"

"It's going to be a Christmas tree. Now don't you laugh. It's not my fault trees don't grow around here. I've got this broomstick, and sticks for branches, and plenty of green crepe paper. Sarah and I are going to make ornaments—we've got cotton and foil and even some glitter."

"Hmm. Very festive," said Steve. "The kids will like it."

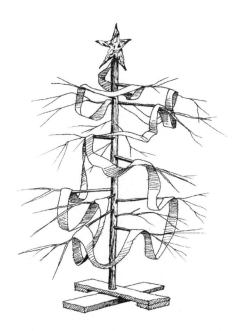

Christmas day came, and dozens of people enjoyed the celebration. They listened attentively to the Christmas story in their own language and sang the new carols again and again. Adults and children alike exclaimed over Liz's Christmas tree. She and Sarah had propped it up on a table and lit it with flashlights so the foil-covered star would shine.

After everyone left, Jackson stayed for one more cup of coffee before he went back to his cold room at the Trading Post. Steve wanted to ask whether he'd had a chance to read the Bible, but he decided to wait for Jackson to bring up the subject.

"This has been really great," said Jackson. "No, not another bite to eat, Liz. What a feast! You even made lima beans and bacon for me. I must admit I've never tasted that kind of pie before. What's in it?"

"Emma gave me her recipe, and Gus got the meat from a herd up at Icy Cape." Liz grinned. "It's reindeer meat and fat, along with dried apples and raisins. Alaskan mincemeat."

"Umm. Well, it tasted good." He sipped at his coffee. "How do you like your new pilot?"

"He seems to be a pleasant sort," said Steve.

"Heard Mack got a job flying for some outfit up North."

"Did he quit?"

"Not exactly. The company suggested that he might like to fly for someone else. There's plenty of jobs for pilots in Alaska. Mack's a good pilot, but I don't know how long he'll last."

"How come?"

Jackson smiled, and his scar glimmered in the lamplight. "Well, you've heard the saying 'There's old pilots and there's bold pilots, but there's no old bold pilots.' ? That's especially true in Alaska." His face sobered. "Mack often boasts about flying whenever he wants to, no matter what the weather. Someday it'll catch up with him."

Jackson looked around the cabin. "I sure do like your Christmas tree, Liz. Too bad your Christmas mail didn't make it in yet. Probably got held up by weather somewhere." He stood to his feet. "That's life in this great Territory, right? Hey, I've got an early flight tomorrow, so I'd better go. Thanks very much, you two."

He put on his flight jacket, then stopped at the cabin door and looked at Steve. "That Bible—I've been reading it now and then. Sometime I'm going to ask you a bunch of questions."

Steve laughed. "I sure don't have all the answers, but I'll do my best. Come back soon."

After the door closed, Liz said, "He's such a nice guy! I can't stand it that he doesn't know Christ."

Steve put an arm around her. "Give him time, Lizzie. And we'll keep praying."

Monday's mail plane brought their Christmas gifts and cards from the States. Liz snatched up a letter from Peter. "Let's save this one for last. He always says good things."

By the time they had opened the gifts and read the cards, Steve felt that Christmas couldn't get much better. He set aside the last card and said, "What I like best is that so many people are praying for Tignak and Charlie and the others. They really care about them."

"Especially Charlie." Liz glanced at the pile of opened mail. "How about that one lady who cried when she heard he'd accepted Christ?"

"Yes," said Steve. "I hope they keep praying. There's still an important battle to be won in his life. He's hanging onto what Am-nok taught him. Every time I see that ivory fox on his parka . . ."

"You want to rip it off," said Liz. "So do I. Here, read me Peter's letter."

"Okay, here's what he says:

*I've got some good news for you. I'm out of the wheelchair these days, walking on my own two feet. The doctor says it's remarkable, but we know Who has been taking care of me. I asked the doctor my big question: WHEN can I go back??? And he said SOON!!! Maybe in March!*

"March!" exclaimed Liz. "He's coming back in March? That's wonderful! Wait til we tell the church!"

The rest of Peter's letter was as encouraging as ever. He was thrilled to hear about Victor's uncle and Henry, and glad Steve had given them each a Bible. He had many comments and questions about Mierow Lake.

Steve folded the letter and put it down on the table. "When Peter comes—"

It hit him suddenly, the joy of knowing that he'd have someone else to share in the ministry. "*When Peter comes! How do you like the sound of that, Lizzie? It's the best Christmas present I could have asked—*" He paused. "Except for . . ."

She met his gaze. "Charlie's amulet?"

"Yes. But I'm so glad that Peter's coming!"

"He'll want to visit Mierow Lake first thing," said Liz. "I wonder what they did for Christmas. Were you thinking about going back soon?"

"Yes, Tignak and I talked about it just yesterday. I really want to give that Bible to Samson, and the people need a lot more teaching."

Steve reached for his parka. "I'll go over now and see what he thinks. Maybe we can leave before another storm swings down the coast."

Tignak agreed to go, and they made plans to leave the next day.

Late that night, Tignak came to their door. His face was drawn, as if in pain. "Our friend Joseph, in Shanaluk, he's very ill. I have to go right away. It may be my last chance to talk to him."

"Sure." Steve's mind raced. "Want me to fly you?"

"No, I'll take my dogs." Tignak smiled faintly. "They travel in any kind of weather, and I can leave before it is light. But about our trip—you'll still go, won't you?"

"I think I'd better."

"How about taking Charlie? He'd be useful, and it might be good for him."

"Great idea. I did promise him, didn't I?" Steve grasped Tignak's hand. "I'll pray for you and Joseph. And you pray for us, okay?"

The next day, Charlie helped Steve preheat the plane and load it with their baggage. Steve checked over the emergency gear, and Charlie set a brown paper package carefully on top of the pile. "Missus Lizzie, she send cookies."

Steve laughed. "Yes, we've got to take good care of those." It was going to be a fine adventure, sharing this trip with Charlie.

By the time they were ready to leave, it was past noon, and they took off under a sun that had risen pale and weak only a few hours before. Steve filed his flight plan and asked for the weather forecast. A storm was coming up the coast later in the day, they said.

*We'll be at Mierow Lake by then,* Steve told himself.

They flew northeast toward the mountains, and Charlie amused himself by looking for animals on the tundra below.

The mountain called Old Man's Hat had just come into sight when Charlie said, "What that?"

A black oily smear was creeping across one corner of the windshield. Steve glanced at the oil pressure gauge. Its needle was dropping.

He snatched up the microphone and tuned in the emergency frequency. "This is Cessna 1577 Zebra. I've got oil coming across my windshield. Doesn't look good. I'm north of Koyalik, approaching Old Man's Hat. 77 Zebra out."

The radio answered with a burst of static.

Steve watched the gauge. With no oil, the engine would freeze up and become a worthless hunk of metal, and the Mission would have to buy a whole new engine. He had to get this plane on the ground before that happened.

By now, thick black oil had covered half the windshield, and the needle on the oil pressure gauge was dropping steadily.

He tried the radio again in hopes that someone would hear. "Cessna 1577 Zebra. Oil pressure dropping fast. I'm going to set this thing down." He glanced out the side window. "Tundra flats below me. Estimate sixty miles north of Koyalik. 77 Zebra out."

Charlie sat frozen in place, and Steve felt a moment of regret that he'd let the boy come along.

But he smiled and said, "Tighten your seat belt. Okay? Now put your arms against the instrument panel and lean forward. Put your head against your arms. Good. In just about a minute, we're going down."

# 14 Zebra in the Snow

Steve glanced again at the windshield. It was completely covered with oil. The oil pressure gauge had fallen to ten.

"That's it." He pulled out the mixture control and shut down the engine. In the sudden silence, all he could hear was wind rushing over the wings. The propeller, faintly visible through the film of oil, turned more and more slowly.

The plane coasted downward. He probably had two minutes before it hit the ground.

He adjusted the trim tabs to get the best airspeed and peered out the side window. The tundra looked fairly level, but under the snow would be hummocks of tough grass and—this close to the mountains—some rocks.

As the plane glided lower and lower, he tried to steer it toward the smoothest possible spot for landing. No time to fly over. No time to check it out.

"Here goes. Sit tight, Charlie."

The plane touched down and slid across the snow. It bounced against something, lurched to the left, tipped up on its nose, and dropped back. The impact threw Steve against the instrument panel and jerked him sideways. Somewhere in his body, something began to hurt.

He glanced at Charlie. The boy was just straightening up, and he seemed to be fine.

Steve leaned against the control wheel and shut his eyes. "Thank you, Lord," he said aloud. "Thank you for keeping Your hand upon us."

He wanted to stay there with his eyes closed until the humming in his head went away, but he made himself sit up and reach for the radio mike. Pain sliced through his right knee. Must have hit that somehow.

He pushed the button on the mike, but the transmit light didn't come on. He pushed it again, harder, and nothing happened. Slowly he put the mike back in its clip. His head began to ache.

"Well, it looks like we've lost our radio." He glanced again at Charlie. "You okay? Sorry about the rough landing."

"Me okay." Charlie gave him a cheerful look that changed to one of concern. "Your head bleeding."

Steve put a hand to his right temple, and it came away smeared with blood. He tried to shake off the mist in front of his eyes. He shifted his position, and pain darted through his knee again.

Charlie gave him another look, wrenched the cockpit door open, and leaped outside. He came back with a handful of snow. "Here, press this."

Steve rested his head against the snow in his mittened hand while Charlie watched him critically.

After a minute, the boy asked, "We have a . . . a . . . box of First?"

"What? Oh. First-aid kit. Yes. In the back."

By the time Charlie returned with bandages, the bleeding had slowed, and Steve let him look at his head.

"Huh," said Charlie. "A cut, not very big. And a bump, getting bigger." He grinned. "I wrap up your head like Gus do."

He bandaged Steve's head securely, and the pain seemed to lessen.

Cold air flooded in from outside, and Steve knew they had to keep moving. "I want to take a look at that engine," he said. "Why don't you start unloading the gear? Maybe set up the tent."

"Sure." Charlie hurried off.

Steve started to leave the cockpit and gasped in pain. He straightened his leg to immobilize that knee, gritted his teeth, and pulled himself out of the plane.

Stiff-legged, he hobbled to the front of the plane and un-latched the cowling.

There it was, a broken flexible oil line. He'd have to get a new one.

His vision blurred as he closed up the cowling, and he had to lean against the fuselage for a minute. He pulled him-self upright and examined the rest of the plane. The pro-peller was bent, the spinner in the middle of the propeller was flattened, and one ski had buckled.

This plane wasn't going anywhere.

A light wind ruffled the fur on his parka and made him glance at the sky. Milky gray clouds were scudding over-head, and the air held a below-zero chill.

Their job was to stay alive until someone found them.

He blinked, trying to clear the haze from his brain. First, tie down the plane. Make sure it's safe. He tried to ignore the pain in his knee and, carefully holding the leg stiff, set to work with stakes and the tie-down ropes. At least there was plenty of snow here.

Charlie had found a small shovel and was carving out snow blocks. By the time Steve finished with the plane, he had dug out a pit in the snow and surrounded it with blocks. The boy looked up, his face mottled red from working in the cold. "For the tent. To keep from wind."

"Great idea," said Steve. Favoring his knee made him clumsy, but he helped Charlie with the snow blocks. Then they unloaded the tent and set it up. Above their harsh breathing came the dry whispering of the wind, growing stronger each minute. At least those snow blocks would give them some protection.

"Storm coming," Charlie said, digging out the last block. He set it in place and eyed the tent. Its wide black stripes stood out boldly against the snow.

He grinned. "Very funny. Zebra in the snow."

Steve started to laugh with him, but the movement made his head throb. Liz had worked hard, sewing on those stripes. He'd have to tell her . . .

Would he ever see Liz again? Had anyone heard his radio transmission?

He glanced at the sky, disappearing now into twilight. Tomorrow, maybe, someone would wonder why he hadn't closed his flight plan. But they couldn't search during a blizzard.

He and Charlie carried the supplies into the tent. It was dim and chilly inside, but it felt almost warm, out of the wind. He tried to think what to do next. "How about something to eat?"

He sent Charlie back out to fill a pot with clean snow while he set up their small stove. His hands ached with cold, and he moved slowly and awkwardly to do a job he had done a hundred times before. He eyed the can of white gas. It wouldn't last more than a couple of days, but maybe that would be long enough.

Charlie crawled back into the tent, his parka dusted with white. "Snow starting," he said without emotion.

It took a long time to melt the snow and cook a meal of hot soup, Spam, and canned potatoes. They spread out their sleeping bags and organized the gear. "No hurry," Charlie said.

Steve had to agree with him. For once, there was no place to go. Cautiously he sat down on his sleeping bag, keeping the bad knee straight. He had swallowed a couple of pain pills with some snow water, so it might feel better soon. It sure was swelling up.

Charlie sat cross-legged on his sleeping bag, eating one of Liz's peanut butter cookies for dessert. "Very good. Missus Lizzie put lots of stuff in cookies. Good for me, she says."

Steve's head was beginning to clear. "Yes, healthy stuff. We'd better not eat them all up today. How many are left?"

Charlie counted. "Ten."

"Okay, what if we make them last for five days?"

"This like school." Charlie frowned. "One cookie for you and one for me each day."

"We'd better do that. And let's divide up the rest of the food. Two meals a day."

"How long?"

Steve hesitated. "Six days?" *Surely by then . . .*

"Look!" Charlie held up three chocolate bars. "We keep for . . . for celebrate?"

"Celebrations?"

"Yes. We will have celebrations."

Daylight faded as the storm grew stronger, and they finished dividing the food and arranging the tent by candlelight. "Let's save our flashlights," said Steve. "The candles should last for a few days if we're careful."

He eased into his sleeping bag. It felt icy inside, with one warm spot where he had been sitting on it, but gradually it warmed around him. He yawned. "I'm going to take a nap, Charlie. You're in charge." He resisted the urge to warn him about staying in the tent. The boy probably knew more about surviving in the wilderness than he ever would.

The throbbing in his head had faded into a dull ache, and he found that if he stayed still, his knee didn't hurt as much. It felt good to close his eyes.

When he awakened, it was dark and very cold. The moisture of his breathing had frozen on the edge of his sleeping bag like heavy frost, and he knocked it off with mittened hands. His knee ached, but his head felt better. What time was it, anyway? He reached for the flashlight, which he kept inside the sleeping bag, and checked his watch. Six o'clock. In the morning? He must have slept all night.

He started to sit up, and pain shot through his knee. He bit back a groan and lay still.

*Try it again. Don't bend that knee.*

Snow flurried against the walls of the tent, and cold hung in the air like something he could touch. Fumbling in the dark and being very careful of his knee, he lit a candle and stuck it upright in a puddle of its own wax, using a can of Spam for a base.

Charlie was curled deep in his sleeping bag, out of sight, like a husky in its snow burrow.

Something hot would taste good.

It seemed to take hours, but finally he got the stove going and melted some snow. Oatmeal and cocoa for breakfast, he decided. Thin oatmeal and thin cocoa, so it would last. He was hungry for more than that, but they'd better save the canned meat.

He banged the ice-cold pans awkwardly as he worked, and Charlie's head appeared. The boy watched him, dark eyes just visible over the edge of his sleeping bag, and Steve wondered what he was thinking. Charlie had changed a lot in the past weeks.

After breakfast, Steve took out his small Bible and looked at Charlie. "Want to hear this?"

"Sure."

The psalm for this day was Psalm 91. Liz would be reading it too, thought Steve. *Lord, give her peace. Protect her from evil.*

Aloud, he read, *"I will say of the Lord, He is my refuge and my fortress: my God; in him will I trust."* He continued on with the rest of the psalm and silently thanked God for His encouragement. "Use this time for Your purposes, Lord," he prayed. "For Charlie?"

Charlie didn't ask any questions, but when they prayed together, he added his own short prayer in English, ending with "Thank You, God, You watch over us."

Then they talked, raising their voices above the sound of the wind that moaned around the tent. Charlie told him how he and Tignak had once taken their boat far up the Yukon River, and Steve described what it was like to grow up in Minnesota. Charlie especially liked hearing how Steve had learned to run his Uncle Alf's dog team. They discussed their favorite dogs, comparing each one with Mikki.

By now they had grown stiff, sitting in the cold, and had to wave their arms and beat their hands together to get warm. Charlie stamped his feet, but Steve knew better than to try moving his knee.

Midafternoon, Steve thought he should check on the airplane, but his knee had swollen so much that he could not bear to walk on it. Charlie crawled outside to look around and get some more snow. He came back almost immediately, covered with white.

"Wind try to knock me down," he said, sounding breathless. "Plane look okay. Snow piled all over."

"Good." Steve had hoped that snow would drift around the plane and keep it from jerking at the ropes. Digging it out would be a big job, but at least it was safe for now.

When the light faded, he lit a candle, and when they grew hungry, he laboriously heated up corned beef and the rest of the potatoes. For dessert, they ate one cookie each. He brewed strong black tea, and while they were drinking it, Steve realized what the date was. "This is New Year's Day!" he exclaimed.

Charlie looked mournful. "Back home they have lotsa games and fun today."

Steve propped up his leg and settled himself as comfortably as he could. "We need to have a celebration for New Year's. Let's split a chocolate bar and you can tell me about that 'lotsa fun.' "

"Yes, yes," said Charlie. He unwrapped a chocolate bar, broke it in half, and handed one piece to Steve. Smiling, he popped one small square of chocolate into his mouth. "Sometimes dog team races," he said. "Then contests. Men lift up other mens to show strong. And kickball. And finger pull."

He leaned forward, his eyes sparkling. "You want to try finger pull?"

Steve looked at Charlie's slender hands. "What do you do?"

"Like this."

Charlie crawled off his sleeping bag and sat facing Steve. He lifted Steve's hand and hooked his index finger around Steve's. "Just pull and see who win."

"Okay." Steve braced his injured knee.

Charlie began to pull, and in less than a minute Steve's finger went straight.

"Do again," Charlie said.

This time it took longer, and Charlie grunted with effort, but Steve's finger straightened once more.

"You pretty good," said Charlie. "Now other fingers."

By the time Charlie was tired of the game, having won most of the bouts, Steve thought his fingers might never bend again. "Congratulations!" He handed the rest of his chocolate bar to Charlie. "For the winner."

Charlie accepted with a grin. "Good thing I win. I already finish mine."

Steve made more tea. This was Wednesday night. Would the men be praying? What would Tignak be doing? How was Joseph? What about Liz? Was it storming in Koyalik? Did anyone know they were down?

With an effort, he turned from the clamoring questions. "Let's get some more exercise!" he said, and pulled himself painfully to his feet. They waved their arms and clapped their hands, trying to get warm. Charlie jumped up and down, keeping to a crouch under the low ceiling. "Good for blood moving," he said with a grin.

When they sat down, Steve suggested that they take turns praying aloud. After Steve was finished, Charlie prayed a long lively prayer in Eskimo, and Steve missed most of it. Would he ever understand this language? That gave him an idea.

"Charlie," he said drowsily, "How about tomorrow we go to school?"

In the shadowy light, Charlie made a sound of astonishment. Or was it dismay?

"Sure," said Steve. "You be the teacher. I need to learn to understand when you talk fast. Okay?"

"Okaaay," Charlie said, and Steve could hear the smile in his voice.

When Steve awoke the next morning, the only thing he could think of was coffee, hot and strong. He lit a candle, then doggedly set about lighting the stove and melting water, mindful of his knee. The thin cocoa didn't taste too bad. At least it was hot.

After another breakfast of oatmeal, he read a psalm and they prayed together. He read a chapter aloud from the Gospel of Mark so Charlie could correct his pronunciation, and after that, they practiced speaking Eskimo until Steve's head began to spin.

Around noon, pale light seeped into the tent, but Steve knew it wouldn't last for long. In December, even in clear weather they didn't get very many hours of daylight.

They both fell silent, listening to the storm, and finally Steve said, "Did I ever tell you about our verse?"

"The one Missus Lizzie color on big piece of paper?"

"Yes. It's from the Book of Joshua. Actually, it's what God said to the great leader Joshua before he set off to conquer the land God had promised them."

Charlie pulled his knife out of his pocket. "What is *conquer?*"

"That's to win, like winning a battle. Joshua and his army fought a lot of battles and won them. God has been showing me that our work here is like being in a battle."

Charlie's dark eyebrows rose. "Who you fight?"

"It's a spiritual battle." Steve paused, praying for the right words to explain.

Charlie nodded and took out his whetstone. He gave Steve an inquiring look, then began sharpening his knife.

"Satan and his forces don't want people to learn about God," said Steve. "He wants people to stay in their sins and be afraid."

Charlie nodded again. "I hear you talk about Satan in church. He fight God. Being scared come from Satan?"

"Yes. You've read about slaves. Doing what Satan wants is like being a slave to a bad king. But Christ came to set people free from evil. And when a person belongs to God instead of to Satan, he doesn't have to be afraid. God will take care of him—like He told Joshua in that verse."

Charlie sighted down his knife. "Tell me verse."

Steve quoted the verse and added, "I've been thinking about that last sentence. *The Lord thy God is with thee whithersover thou goest.* It still amazes me. God is right here with us, now. And He's with Liz back in Koyalik, and with your father, visiting in Shanaluk. Jesus said the same thing when He told His friends, *Lo, I am with you alway, even unto the end of the world."*

Charlie leaned over and tapped the Gospel of Mark with his knife. "Where Jesus say that?"

"Well, it's not in Mark. It's in another book of the Bible called Matthew."

"Oh." Charlie was silent for a minute. "Did God write the Bible in English?"

"No." Steve had to smile. "No, He told some men the words to write and they wrote in their own language."

"What language?"

"Some wrote in Hebrew, some in Aramaic, some in Greek."

"Strange names."

"Then some people translated the Greek words, for example, into other languages like English. And now into Eskimo. Hey, I know what we could do." Steve sat up, jerking his knee. He had to stop and rub it for a minute.

"What?"

"You could help me translate that Joshua verse into Eskimo. How about it?"

"Okay, how do it go?"

Steve's pen had frozen, so he used a pencil, and they started on a rough Eskimo translation of Joshua 1:9. As they worked, Steve prayed that Charlie would begin to understand what it said.

Charlie wrote on the brown paper Liz had wrapped around the cookies, and the smell of them made Steve hungry again. The wind howled outside, buffeting the tent with gusts of snow. Steve thought about the Cessna and tried not to worry. *It's Your plane, Lord,* he prayed silently. *Keep Your hand upon it and on us too.*

Although daylight soon faded, they worked by candle-light, stopping often to discuss the meaning of a word. Steve's stomach began to grumble, so he cooked dried peas for supper and flavored them with corned beef and an enve-lope of dried beef soup. Steve ate his plateful very slowly to make it last. Charlie was doing the same.

"How come you eat these little round things?" asked Charlie.

"Dried peas? They're easy to pack and cook, and they have lots of fiber and protein in them, to keep us strong."

"You sound like Missus Lizzie," said Charlie. "When we get back, first thing I want big plate muktuk. Then some good fat caribou."

"Caribou steak for me," said Steve. "With onions and gravy."

He blew out the candles, and they talked in the darkness for a while. Then they each prayed aloud, as before.

Steve awoke several times during the night, shivering. It must be getting colder. The shivering sent twinges of pain through his knee, and while he was trying to get comfort-able, he knocked the bandage off his head. The cut seemed okay, though. He'd just have to be careful not to hit it again.

He curled up and tried to sleep some more, but his feet had turned to ice. *I should have brought Mikki,* he thought drowsily. An airplane is fine for transportation, but you sure couldn't snuggle up to one.

He checked his watch. It was early morning now, but the tent was still dark, and the storm still howled outside.

# 15 Whithersoever

The next time Steve awoke, the walls of the tent had lightened to pale gray. His cheeks and the end of his nose ached with cold. He imagined pouring himself a cup of coffee—an oversized, piping hot cup of coffee, with lots of sugar and cream. He would pick it up, and it would warm his hands. The steam would rise into his face, and it would taste so smooth, so satisfying, going down his throat.

*The next time I pack for a trip,* he thought, *I'm sure going to put in some coffee.*

He pulled the food box closer to his sleeping bag, and Charlie sat up, yawning. Steve peered into the box. "I think we need a special breakfast," he said. "How about a raisin cake?"

Charlie's eyes widened. "Cake?"

"You know: mix flour and eggs and sugar and raisins and cinnamon and bake it in a round pan."

Charlie looked interested, and Steve grinned at him. "I don't have any flour or eggs or cinnamon. And we're almost out of sugar. But I've got raisins. And just for you, since you're my best customer, I'll throw them into a nice big pot of oatmeal."

Charlie smiled, understanding. "Raisins, good."

Steve pumped the little stove so he could light its burners, but nothing happened. Now what?

He looked inside the reservoir and found that the fuel moved as slowly as catsup. Frozen. The can of white gas was frozen too. He'd known they didn't have a lot of fuel, but he wasn't ready for this.

"Well, Charlie, we'll have to postpone our pot of oatmeal."

He didn't want to use the flashlight or the candles any more than necessary, so they peered through the gloom at their food supplies. What didn't need to be cooked? The canned meat had frozen into bricks, but there were raisins, and the frozen bannock could be broken up. One cookie for each.

"We could share a chocolate bar too," said Steve.

Charlie grinned. "Celebration for coldest day of year? Okay."

There was nothing to drink, since the snow water had frozen solid. Steve allowed them each some snow to suck on, but only a small bit. He explained to Charlie that it was dangerous to eat snow because it took so much body heat to melt. Charlie nodded, as if he knew that already.

When a little more light crept into the tent, they finished translating the verse and memorized it in both English and Eskimo.

A long silence fell, broken only by the hiss of snow against the tent. Charlie stared at the stripes on the ceiling of the tent. Steve decided to organize his duffle bag, and he dumped out its contents. The red Bible he'd packed for Samson slid out onto his sleeping bag, and Charlie pounced on it.

He opened the book and leafed through a few pages. "Lotsa big words. Soon I can read big English words too. How come you got two Bibles?"

Steve told him how Peter had sent them the Bibles and about Samson at Mierow Lake.

Charlie nodded. "Samson be happy to get this. But not yet okay?"

Steve had to smile at the way he'd said it. "Not yet okay. God knows the right time for Samson to get that Bible. I can wait."

Once again, he had been prevented from getting to Mierow Lake. Was the Enemy trying to discourage him? But God had a purpose in allowing this delay. *Not yet okay, Lord.* He whistled softly to himself as he finished repacking the duffle bag.

What could they do next? "Hey, Charlie, let's sing," he said. "We can celebrate with songs because we did such good work on that verse."

He gave a regretful glance at their tea bags. Something hot to drink would be really nice to have right now. Could they start a fire with gas from the plane? Possibly, but a person could freeze to death just trying to get at the gas.

They sang for a while, wrapped in their sleeping bags since the tent was so cold. When their voices grew hoarse, they ate more raisins and the last of the bannock and went to bed early.

At first Steve couldn't get to sleep. He tossed and turned, trying to get warm without banging his knee. He was hungry too. That bannock would have been good dipped into some of Liz's caribou stew. He pretended he was writing Liz a long letter and fell asleep missing her.

When morning light finally came, he welcomed it, cold and pale though it was. He checked the can of white gas. Still frozen.

"Hey. You hear that?" Charlie said, his voice rasping with cold.

"What?" The word came out as a croak.

"The wind. It change. Maybe weather change too." Charlie sat up and struggled out of his sleeping bag. "I go see. Get some snow too."

While he was gone, Steve listened to the wind, trying to figure out how it sounded different, but he couldn't tell. Gingerly, he flexed his knee. Not as swollen, but it still hurt. He had managed to sit up and light a candle by the time Charlie returned.

Charlie stooped to put down the pan of snow.

There was something different about the boy's parka. What was it?

Steve blinked and looked again. The small ivory fox was gone.

He handed Charlie the candle and stayed calm with an effort. "What happened to that fox carving of yours?"

"Oh." Charlie's eyes sparkled. "Last night I throw it into snow."

"Why'd you do that?"

Charlie sat down cross-legged and put his hands inside his parka to warm them. "You belong to Christ. Me too. I not slave to evil. I watch you. God go with you everywhere. You talk to Him—not scared. You not need a fox to help you." He smiled. "God go with me, just like you. Now I not scared. I want to fight battle too."

The candle flame blurred before Steve's eyes. "That's great news, Charlie! Wonderful! God will bless you for trusting Him."

*Lord,* he thought, *no matter what happens, You have made me the happiest man in the world today.*

"Hey," he said, "I think we should celebrate with that last chocolate bar for breakfast." He grinned to see Charlie dive for the chocolate bar and unwrap it.

"Good news," said Charlie. He used his knife to shave a stiff little curl off his piece of frozen chocolate.

"Yes, it sure is," said Steve.

Charlie gave him a puzzled look. "No, about the storm. Going away."

"The storm?" Steve pulled his thoughts together. "Oh, good!"

It stopped snowing at about noon, and they crawled outside. Steve brushed the snow off the top of the tent, thankful for those distinctive black stripes. Charlie headed off toward some sticks that poked up from the drifts. He returned with an armful of willow branches.

"Now we can make a fire!" exclaimed Steve. Something hot to drink! In his excitement he dropped the matches and had to dig for them in the soft snow.

He collected some gas from the sump drain in one wing of the plane and used it to start the fire. A wispy thread of black smoke rose into the air. It was too small for anyone to see, but at least they could melt snow.

He limped behind Charlie to get more branches, and they piled up a stack for later. Then they made tea and a hearty soup thickened with dried peas.

Charlie stared to the south, across the glistening expanse of white tundra. "Okay, now storm stop, we go."

Steve looked up from his soup in alarm. "What do you mean?"

"You think we sixty miles from Koyalik?"

"That's my guess."

"We can walk. Take a few days maybe. Shoot rabbits on the way." Charlie's breath turned to ice particles on the ruff of his parka. "Better than wait here and no food left. Maybe they never find us."

"I understand what you're saying, but the rule is to stay with the plane. A plane is easier to see than a couple of people, especially in all this snow. And we have the zebra tent."

Charlie did not look convinced. "How come you so sure they find us? Plane very small. Covered with snow. Tent very small. Can they see one little zebra in all this snow?"

"Now that the storm's gone, we can make a signal fire," said Steve. "And brush off the airplane. Jackson knows our route, and he'll come looking for us."

"But he not know we take this trip." Charlie kicked at the snow, looking stubborn. "You got bad knee. Maybe I go."

"Don't," said Steve. "It never works to split up. Please, Charlie, don't try it. Come on, let's get to work on this plane."

It took more than an hour to clear off the Cessna because they had to rub a heavy rope, seesaw fashion, across the tops of the wings until the wind-driven snow broke loose. Steve's lungs burned from the icy air, and their breath hung in clouds of vapor above them, white against the frozen blue sky.

"We need to fix a place for someone to land," said Steve. He let Charlie use his snowshoes, and the boy tramped down the snow for a short runway, checking for rocks as he went.

When that was done, they gathered more branches. By sunset, Steve's knee throbbed with pain, and he felt as if he could not drag himself one step farther.

That evening they talked quietly in the icy darkness of the tent.

"Can fix airplane?" asked Charlie.

"Yes, but we'll have to take the propeller to Nome and get it straightened out. And buy some parts—a new spinner and a new oil line."

"Fix ski?"

"No, I guess not. We'll have to buy a new ski too."

Steve pulled himself slowly and painfully to his feet. "I'm about frozen. Wish I could jump up and down."

"Better we make more fire, get warm," said Charlie.

"Okay." Steve hated to use up their supply of branches, but his hands were so cold he could barely manage the zipper on the tent. "Maybe a small fire."

The wind had dropped, and the flames went straight up. The fire warmed Steve's face, but it left the harsh cold of his back untouched. He turned and stretched to soak up the heat. He glanced overhead.

"Look at that, Charlie! Look what God made for us!" The Big Dipper was huge in the sky above them. The Northern Lights swept glittering white beams across the stars and sent gauzy curtains of red and green swirling in every direction.

Charlie stared up at the sky. "How you know God make stars?"

"The Bible talks about it. The Book of John says, *All things were made by him; and without him was not any thing made that was made.*" It was one of the verses he'd memorized with Tignak, and he repeated it in Eskimo: "*Itlekun piortsimalra tamatikuan piortlrok; itlengunrilingorkundlo tsha mana piortlrunritok.*"

"Is a very great God," said Charlie.

They stamped their feet and waved their arms, and Steve's body warmed in patches, tingling. When the fire burned down, they crept back into the tent and their cold sleeping bags.

The hours passed slowly, as if they too were frozen.

An icy chill rose in his bones, and Steve realized for the first time how easy it would be to die of cold. Just drift off, float away . . .

He pulled himself into a tight ball. No, he wasn't going to let that happen. His knee ached, and he wished he'd been more careful with it. The days ahead were going to be hard enough without having a crippled knee. He rubbed it, praying that God would send someone soon, and thanking Him again for setting Charlie free.

*Make him a strong soldier, Lord.*

He slid in and out of drowsiness, shivering, for most of the night. Finally he slept, and he awoke to find that the walls of the tent had lightened. He leaned up on one elbow to see how Charlie was doing. His sleeping bag was empty.

Had he decided to take off on his own?

Steve dragged himself to the door of the tent. He'd never be able to catch up with the boy.

Charlie looked up from where he stood beside a small fire, feeding it branches. "I think you sleep all day."

*Thank you, Lord.*

He turned back into the tent for his mittens and accidentally knocked over the can of white gas. As he set it upright, he heard a liquid, sloshing sound.

*Thank you again, Lord!*

He pumped up the stove, and soon they were drinking hot cocoa in the pale dawn and discussing what to eat for breakfast. Steve kept the portions small, since they didn't knew how long the food would have to last, but at least they had plenty to drink.

"Now I get more wood." Charlie turned to leave, and the sound of an airplane engine hummed overhead.

It was a twin engine plane, flying high, and it kept going.

"Let's build the biggest fire we can," said Steve. "Maybe he'll come back. Or someone else will fly over. I'm sure they're looking for us."

After the fire was lit and a towering column of black smoke rose into the sky, Charlie got out the shovel and began cutting blocks of snow.

"What's that for?"

"We build a wall. Jackson tell me. It make a shadow they can see—not look like anything else."

Steve grabbed a block of snow to lift it into place and almost fell over. He straightened up, his legs shaky, his knee sending him warning twinges of pain.

He'd have to move a little more slowly. And watch that knee.

It took hours, both of them stumbling and exhausted, before the wall was done. It curved crazily, but it stood as tall as Steve and at least eight feet long. The sun had risen slowly behind them, and long black shadows stretched in front of the wall.

"Not bad," said Steve. He brushed ice from the ruff of his parka. "That should grab their attention."

They dug away some of the snow that had drifted under the Cessna's wings, then made a cup of tea and climbed into the plane to drink it.

"A change from the tent," said Steve. But it was bitterly cold in here.

"Yes—" Charlie stopped himself. "You hear some-thing?"

"No." But Steve slid out of the airplane, banging his knee on the door. He dropped his cup in the snow and stood beside the plane, waving his arms and yelling.

High above them flew something that looked like a yel-low mosquito. It circled lower and lower, then dipped a wing.

"Jackson!" shouted Charlie.

The Piper Cub zoomed over their heads and made a wide circle, turning back toward them.

Charlie jumped up and down. "He find us! *God* tell him where we are. Because *tangerlukodlo nayortlainaramtse tlam ekuktlitdlerkan ngilenu!*"

Steve grinned. "You said it! *Whithersoever thou goest.*"

The Cub flew low over their makeshift runway, then it turned and lined up for the final approach. It glided lower and lower, yellow wings gleaming, and touched down in a spray of glittering white.

Steve hobbled forward, and Charlie ran shouting to meet it.